The World Spins Madly On

Caroline T. Patti

iUniverse, Inc.
New York   Bloomington

The World Spins Madly On

Copyright © 2008 by Caroline T. Patti

iUniverse books may be ordered through booksellers or by contacting:

iUniverse
1663 Liberty Drive
Bloomington, IN 47403
www.iuniverse.com
1-800-Authors (1-800-288-4677)

ISBN: 978-0-595-47439-4 (pbk)
ISBN: 978-0-595-71087-4 (cloth)
ISBN: 978-0-595-91716-7 (ebk)

Printed in the United States of America

To Matt Maes and Brian Phipps—
because I always said I would.

ACKNOWLEDGMENTS

I would like to thank John Hesse Jr. for giving me the loving nudge I needed to get started. To my wonderful and patient husband, John Hesse III, thank you for all of your assistance and guidance. To all of you who read and reread countless drafts, especially Jennifer Toy, my gratitude is immeasurable. Thank you especially to Joseph and Leslie Patti, my parents, for their love and support.

To all of those at iUniverse who worked with me on this project and guided me in the right direction, I am very grateful.

Lastly, I would like to thank my daughters, Isabelle and Madelyn, for letting Mommy work.

PART ONE
NETTIE

CHAPTER ONE
THE ANNIVERSARY

Buzz! Buzz! Nettie's alarm clock blared. Sluggishly she rolled over to check the time: 7:30. *Time to get up and face the day.* Kicking off the covers of her small twin bed, leaving them in a crumpled heap at the bottom, Nettie trudged to the bathroom. Just as she was about to open the door she hesitated. She remembered that today was not just any other day. Today was the kind of day to make her bed without being asked. Quickly she did an about face. She pulled the sheets straight, shoving the loose ends under the mattress. She smoothed out the frilly pink bedspread. Lastly she returned the decorative pillows to their correct resting place. Stepping back to inspect her work, Nettie frowned. Her room was still the room of a ten-year-old girl. Teddy bears huddled together on the armchair in the corner. Posters of unicorns and fairies stared back at her from her lavender-colored walls. It was as if time stood still in this room. Time stood still in other rooms in the house as well, but Nettie preferred not to think about that. She made a mental note to ask her mother if they might update her room. *Today is my birthday,* Nettie thought to herself, *and I'm a teenager now. I definitely need to make my room more sophisticated.*

Nettie turned on the shower and waited for the water to get warm. She brushed her teeth. Her braces, which had been removed two weeks earlier, left her teeth feeling a bit slimy. She ran her tongue along the front of her cleaned teeth and smiled. She turned to the side to inspect her profile. She pulled the back of her nightshirt tightly against herself and examined her silhouette. Unlike most of the girls in her class, Nettie was developing slowly. Her nonexistent chest and slim hips left her looking a bit boyish. Nettie sighed and let go of her nightshirt.

1

Freshly showered and hair blown dry, Nettie swung open her closet's double doors and contemplated its contents. She never knew what to wear to this sort of thing. At first she thought she should wear black, but she hated that idea. For one thing, it was summer, well, the end of summer anyway, and black would be too hot. For another thing, it was her birthday too, and she didn't feel like dressing like a mourner. But she didn't want to be disrespectful either. In the end she chose a khaki skirt, navy blue polo shirt, and brown sandals. She pulled her hair back into a ponytail and was about to fasten her watch when her mother called from downstairs.

"Nettie! Phone."

"Coming!" Nettie yelled back.

Nettie picked the phone up off the counter. "Hello."

"Hey," Elisa said. "Happy birthday! How are you?"

"Fine. What's up?" Nettie knew her best friend too well. This was not the usual birthday call from one best friend to another. This was the pity call. Nettie appreciated the sentiment and she knew that Elisa was just trying to help, but just once she wanted her birthday to be just about her. For years now a shadow had hung over the day, a constant reminder that this day would never just be about Nettie. Secretly, Nettie hated that it could never just be her birthday. She hoped that didn't make her selfish.

"Are we still hanging out tonight?" Elisa asked.

"Of course. We're leaving in a few minutes and then we'll go to brunch and a movie like we always do. I'll call you when we get home."

"Sounds good. You sure you're okay?"

Nettie shifted uncomfortably from one foot to another. She hated being pitied, especially by her best friend. "I'm fine."

"Okay."

Nettie fidgeted with her glasses. She heard the car engine start. "I've gotta go, my Mom's waiting."

"I'll talk to you soon," Elisa said. "If you need anything I'm here."

"Thanks. I'm fine though, really. I'll talk to you later. Bye." Nettie hung up the phone without waiting to hear Elisa say good-bye.

Nettie stopped to check herself in the hall mirror. After dabbing cherry lip gloss to her lips, she gave herself one last good look. *It'll have to do.* She grabbed the dozen white roses from the hall table and headed out to the car.

Nettie spent most of the drive staring out the window. She reached for the radio dial, thought better of it, and retracted her arm. On most occasions Nettie loved riding in the car with her mom. They would turn the radio to KABL, the oldie but goodie station, and sing along to what her mom called "the classics." Occasionally, the radio station played a hit by Nettie Lu Turner, the "Soul of the Bay," as she was known in her day. Nettie knew that even the sweet sound of her great-grandmother's voice would not be comforting today.

Annie Gaines gripped the steering wheel with white knuckles. She let out a sigh. "Thanks for doing this with me." She turned to Nettie and did her best to force a grin. "No problem," Nettie answered.

For the past three years, on August 21, Nettie and her mother made the same drive to the same place. Each year her mother drove the same route as if on automatic pilot. Sycamore Street, left on Fifth, past Trinity Church and the Nineteenth Street Theater until the road gradually veered right and ended at the T intersection of Fifth and Main. Nettie knew the drive by heart. She knew every house and every giant willow tree.

Annie made a tight left turn through the narrow opening between the two huge gates. The gates never changed. Neither did the sign they held: Forever Peace Children's Cemetery. She slowed the car and gently pulled up next to the curb.

"We're here," Annie said in a voice barely above a whisper. She said the same thing every year as she turned off the car. Nettie knew she wasn't really saying it to her. She said it to brace herself.

Nettie opened the car door and stepped out into the cool summer morning. The once green hills were dried brown in the summer heat. Nettie wished her brother had been born in the spring. If he'd been born in May or June, then flowers would cover the hillside. If Joe's grave was on a pretty, flower-covered hill, then Nettie could imagine him resting somewhere beautiful. As it was it depressed Nettie to think of Joe buried here, without flowers, without the smell of blossoms. He deserved better.

"Are you coming?" Nettie did not realize her mom was out of the car and halfway up the hill. She hurried to catch up. Together they walked across the lawn. As she walked, Nettie scanned the surrounding headstones, each marking a tragic day when a child's life was cut short. Molly Jane Suthers July 7, 1981–April 20, 1987. Adam Louis Cummings December 3, 1992–March 30, 2004.

At last they found the spot they were looking for.

Joseph Matthew Gaines 1988–2004

Beloved Son and Brother.

Once a Superstar Among Us,

Now an Angel Above Us.

Annie knelt down and brushed the leaves from the top of the headstone. "Happy birthday, baby." He would have been nineteen this year.

Nettie looked down at her mother. Tears stained her cheeks. They sat together in silence for a few moments. Annie looked around the cemetery. Nettie knew what her mother was thinking. Nettie was thinking the same thing. *Maybe this year he'll come.* But he didn't come. He never came. Nettie had no idea if her father ever visited Joe's grave. Nettie hadn't heard from or seen her father in almost two years.

Annie made the sign of the cross and said a prayer. When she was done, she brushed away more leaves, but it made no difference. Clean or dirty it was still a grave.

"Shall we go?" Annie asked. She rose from the ground and dusted off her pants. Nettie remained seated.

"Um, just a sec, okay?" Nettie asked.

"Sure kiddo. I'll wait for you in the car." Annie turned and walked down the hill looking back only once.

Nettie sat for a few moments. Tears welled behind her eyes. She fought them off. She would not cry, not today. She would just talk, like she always had, to her older brother.

"Hey, Joe." Nettie laid the roses she'd been carrying on the grass. "I brought you flowers. White roses, just like you used to give me on our birthday. I'm thirteen. A teenager, finally." Nettie looked down at her bony body and shrugged. "I suppose I don't look much like one, though."

Nettie removed her glasses and wiped her eyes with the back of her hand. She stiffened. *Don't cry. Don't be sad. Joe would hate that.* She quickly thought of something light to say. "Football season starts in a few weeks. Mom and I still watch all the games. It's not the same without you, though. Half the time I have no idea what's happening. I should've listened to you all the times you tried to explain football to me. I guess I wasn't always the greatest little sister."

One tear broke through, weaving down her face and coming to rest for a moment on her cheek before she wiped it away. She wondered if she'd ever get used to this, visiting a grave. It barely seemed possible that Joe had been gone for three years. It felt like yesterday they were laughing, talking. This wasn't supposed to happen. Life was not supposed to stop after only sixteen years. Nettie grew angry at the injustice of it all. It wasn't fair. She wished there was someone to complain to, to yell at, but there was no one. There was nothing left of Joe except memories. There was nothing left of the life she once knew and loved.

"I really miss you Joe," Nettie whispered. "Do you miss me?" She hesitated, secretly waiting for an answer or some kind of sign. The silence that filled the air around her was suffocating.

"I start eighth grade next week. I wish I could say I'm looking forward to it, but I'm not. It'll probably be just like all the rest, a total disaster. I'm just really hoping I can survive this year without too much embarrassment." She paused. "Of course that won't happen. I'll probably be the only kid in junior high who isn't asked to the Grad Dance. Not that I mind that much," she lied. "I've pretty much gotten used to the idea that Andrew and I are never going to be boyfriend and girlfriend." Nettie thought back to when she was ten and all was right with the world. She was just a kid, but she knew even then that she would only ever love one person, Andrew Wyatt.

"I guess it was stupid of me to think he and I were somehow destined to be together. But it would've been so perfect. I mean you were dating his older sister and you guys were so in love. I just thought the same thing would happen for Andrew and me. I was so wrong. By now I should know that nothing works out the way I think it's going to."

Nettie wiped her eyes again and said, "If it did I obviously wouldn't be here. Mom's waiting, I should go." Nettie turned away from the grave. She stopped, turned back and whispered, "Happy birthday, Joe."

Nettie made the lonely walk down the hill to the car. The hairs on the back of her neck stood up. Suddenly she had the feeling she was not alone. She looked around but saw no one. She shivered and kept walking down the hill. Once in the car, Nettie turned toward the window. She pressed her forehead to the glass, watching her warm breath leave imprints of hollow circles. Her mother reached over and stroked her hair. In silence they drove, retracing their familiar route.

Annie stopped the car on Main Street in front of a newly-opened café. "Why don't we try it out?"

It wasn't like her mother to deter from their normal routine. The idea of trying something new intrigued Nettie. If her mother was ready to make a change, asking her to redecorate her bedroom might not be as difficult as Nettie first thought.

It would be good for them to try and move on. Whatever that meant. For a while now friends and family had been whispering about moving forward. They needed to get on with their lives, or so they'd been told. The concept never felt quite right to Nettie. Moving forward felt more like forgetting, and that was impossible.

Annie pulled into the parking lot and parked the car. The restaurant looked inviting. The café was actually an old Victorian house with freshly-painted white shutters and a bright red door. The sign read Red Door Café. An array of flowers bloomed in topiaries near the front door. They climbed the steps, and just as Annie reached for the front door, it opened.

"Annie. Hi." A tall man with a decently muscular build stood before them. His shaggy hair hung loosely over his left eye, which he brushed away.

"Chris. This is a surprise." Annie blushed. "Nettie, this is your new teacher, Chris, I mean Mr. Campbell."

"We met on parent's night," Mr. Campbell added quickly.

"Hi," Nettie muttered.

"It's nice to meet you, Nettie. I've heard lots about you."

"Really? Why?" Nettie asked nervously.

Mr. Campbell simply chuckled. "I look forward to seeing you in class next week."

Nettie nodded at his politeness. "Mom, should we go inside?"

"Oh right," Annie said, a bit startled. "It's Nettie's birthday."

"Right. Happy birthday, Nettie."

"Thank you," Nettie answered politely.

"Well, Chr … Mr. Campbell it was very nice running into you. I'm sure we'll see you again." Annie smiled widely.

"It was great seeing you. Both," Mr. Campbell added, "Enjoy your brunch. And again, happy birthday, Nettie." He walked past them out into the parking lot.

That was weird, Nettie thought.

CHAPTER TWO

THE TRYOUT

Nettie stood outside of the gym, hesitant to enter. The flyer taped to the door read, "Volleyball tryouts today 10:30. Don't forget your kneepads!" Nettie's hands began to sweat and her heartbeat quickened. She'd never tried out for any kind of team before. Against her better judgment she'd let Elisa talk her into this. She wondered if she could back out of it.

Elisa walked up behind her. "You ready? I need to get to my PE locker to change clothes." Elisa and Nettie, best friends since kindergarten, were almost inseparable. They liked the same books, the same movies, the same boys. They finished each other's sentences, always knowing what the other was thinking. Unlike Nettie, Elisa was an athlete. At five feet nine inches tall with a muscular body, Elisa looked much older than her actual age. Her cascading red curls framed her creamy white face. Her aqua eyes were without a doubt the feature that everyone noticed first, followed closely by her rolling curves—a body that Nettie envied.

"Why am I doing this again?" Nettie whined as she followed Elisa to the locker room.

"Because you're my best friend and I think it will be fun," Elisa answered.

"As much fun as rollerblading last weekend?" Nettie said as she raised an eyebrow at her friend.

"Yeah, you did fall down a lot. But this will be different." Elisa smiled. "Everyone who tries out makes the team, and I just thought this would be something we could do together. You know I don't really like anyone else on the team. I need my best friend."

Nettie laughed as Elisa gave her signature puppy dog eyes and pouting lip. She threw her hands up in surrender. "Okay, okay. I'll do it. But you owe me. Big time."

In the locker room the girls changed into their volleyball outfits. Elisa looked the part perfectly with her boy shorts, two overlapping tank tops, and kneepads. Nettie felt more than slightly out of place. All around her Nettie heard sounds of laughter, of girls having fun. They were not nervous. They did not have any reason to be. They were athletes. Unlike Nettie.

Nettie had been born athletically deficient. She was awkward, gangly, and uneasy on her feet. Normally, Nettie would not agree to try out for any sport. Elisa had been trying for a few years now to get Nettie to play volleyball, and until recently, she'd always refused. Nettie figured it was easier to sit on the sidelines and watch than to step onto the court and risk humiliation. She did that enough just walking around. Deep down, however, Nettie wished things were different. That's why she agreed to try out. She wanted desperately to believe that she really was more like her brother. He was an athlete, he was popular, and he was smart. So far, Nettie was only one out of three. She hoped today would be her day. Today just might be the day she showed herself, and all the other girls in her class, that she wasn't just a nerd.

Nettie took a deep breath and said a little prayer as she followed the other girls into the gym.

"Okay girls! On the baseline, please. I'm going to divide you into two teams," yelled Mr. Garwitch, the PE teacher and volleyball coach. Reading from his clipboard he continued, "When I call your name, step onto the court. Anna Winchester, Drew Summers, Jacey Parks, Mila Juarez, Cassie Alington, and," he paused, "Nettie Gaines?" He looked up to make sure. The rest of the girls looked around. Suddenly all eyes were on her. Nettie tugged at the bottom of her shirt trying not to catch anyone's gaze. "You're on this side, receiving. Samantha Minor, Elisa Evans, Lanie Donovan, Gwen Chillery, Valerie Bruno, and Julie Hathaway, you're on the other side, serving. Okay, let's go!" Mr. Garwitch slapped the clipboard, signaling to everyone to take their places.

Nettie stepped onto the court. She wiped her hands along her shorts hoping to dry off the sweat that was rapidly accumulating on her palms.

Samantha stepped back to the line and perched the ball on her outstretched left hand. With one swift motion she tossed the ball into the air and served. Nettie watched anxiously as the ball sailed over the net.

It was not coming to her.

Thank God.

Anna stepped forward, calling "Mine!" She clasped her hands together in front of her, making a perfect platform and passed the ball to Drew, the setter.

Drew raised her hands in the air and set the ball to Jacey, the tallest girl in school. Jacey made her approach with long and steady strides. Her hand hit the ball with a loud whack. The ball made a perfect downward spiral over the net.

Samantha and Lanie launched themselves forward in a dramatic, diving attempt to scoop up the ball. But Jacey's hit was too powerful and the ball bounced between them as they came crashing to the floor.

Side out.

Now it was Nettie's team's turn to serve. As Mila stepped back to the serving line, Nettie felt exhilarated. *Finally, I'm on a winning team.*

Mila's serve floated easily over the net. Gwen stepped forward, arms extended, and passed to Valerie, who set to Julie.

As Julie made her approach Nettie readied herself. Leaning forward slightly, she put all her weight on the balls of her feet. The ball angled itself toward her.

"I got it!" Nettie yelled. She took two small steps forward toward the ball and held her arms in front of her. *I can do this. I can do this.*

All at once, Nettie realized her mistake. She was too close to the ball.

Before she could readjust her position the ball hit her square in the nose and she went down like a chopped tree. Nettie imagined someone yelling, "Timber!" as she hit the floor. She lay on the gym floor for several seconds in pain, astonished and humiliated.

"Smooth." Her teammate Mila glared down at her.

"So pathetic," Drew Summers hissed to her teammates. They giggled.

Elisa jogged over to Nettie. Nettie grabbed Elisa's hand and peeled herself off the gym floor.

"Okay, so I was wrong. Sports are not your thing," Elisa smiled.

"I told you." Nettie wiped her hands and checked her nose. At least it wasn't broken.

"When tryouts are over I'll buy you frozen yogurt and make it up to you," Elisa offered.

"Deal. Now can I please leave?" Nettie pleaded.

"I think you better while your head is still attached to your body." Elisa laughed.

Nettie couldn't help but laugh. "See you later," she said as she walked off the court.

Chapter Three

The Beginning of the Year

F ive minutes before the first bell, the eighth grade class at St. Elizabeth's lined up on the blacktop outside the classroom. Girls in plaid skirts and white polo shirts clutched the latest bags, Kate Spade messenger bags mostly. Backpacks were "so sixth grade," according to Drew Summers, the most popular and evil girl in school. Boys in brown corduroys donned a variety of baseball hats sporting logos of their favorite teams, hats they were forced to remove once class commenced.

Nettie stood toward the back of the line, a copy of *The Sisterhood of the Traveling Pants* perched perfectly between her two hands. Her backpack fit snugly against her body, her blonde hair pulled back into a high tight ponytail. Engrossed in her reading, Nettie did not notice Elisa standing next to her.

"Hey!" Elisa said. Nettie nearly jumped out of her skin, "Good book?" Elisa smiled at her friend's ability to concentrate on a book while oblivious to the world around her.

"Yeah. It's good. How was your weekend?"

"Good. Mostly I helped my mom around her shop."

"That's cool."

"Oh yeah, sweeping hair in a salon is just so glamorous." Elisa mockingly swished her hair around her shoulders. "What'd you do this weekend?"

"Not much. Hung out. Read. The usual."

"Wow Nettie. You should slow down. Take it easy with all the partying or you'll end up in rehab with Lindsay Lohan."

"Very funny." Nettie playfully nudged her best friend.

"So have you heard anything about the new teacher?"

"I actually met him."

"Seriously?" Elisa's eyes grew wide. "When?"

"On my birthday."

"And you're just telling me now? What gives? Give me the 411."

"There's not much to tell. He seems normal." Nettie muttered to herself, "Sure likes my mom."

"*What?*" Elisa looked like she could fall over.

"Not like that. They met at parent's night I guess. And then we saw him at The Red Door Café on my birthday and he was all smiley and she was all goofy."

"God, don't you hate watching your parents around teachers? You can never quite tell who's kissing whose butt."

The bell rang, interrupting their conversation. The door to the classroom opened. Mr. Campbell stood tall in a typical teacher's outfit—Dockers, button-down white shirt with the sleeves rolled up, and a blue-and-yellow striped tie. His hair was combed more properly than it had been the other day at the café. He wore the same smile, though—cheerful, optimistic. Nettie felt a little pang of pity for him. He had no idea what he was getting himself into.

Eighth graders were notoriously trouble, with stubborn boys who needed to prove their masculinity, and girls who needed to show off their sass. Nettie's class was no exception. *He'll see soon enough*, Nettie thought.

"Hey, I thought parent's night was this Thursday?" Elisa asked as they entered the classroom.

"What?" Nettie tried to ask, but Mr. Campbell was already giving out instructions.

"Good morning, class," Mr. Campbell said in an authoritative voice. "Welcome to the beginning of an exciting new journey." Nettie could feel twenty-seven pairs of eyes rolling back into their heads.

"This year we are going to learn a lot of exciting new things. We'll explore the worlds of Arthur Miller, Harper Lee, and Shakespeare. We'll begin pre-algebra, world geography and cultures, as well as embark on a personal spiritual journey. I invite you now to pick any seat in the class. This will be your temporary seat for the next four weeks. Choose wisely."

The entire class looked around at one another, trying to decipher Mr. Campbell's last comment. It was highly unusual for a teacher to allow students free reign over seating assignments. This was after all a private, Catholic school. Students were expected to follow the rules of the school as well as the Lord. Free choice was not something they were granted easily. St. Elizabeth's was a place where "Children learn to follow and lead in the path of Jesus Christ." At least that's what it said on the school's crest. In Nettie's experience, most teachers were overly strict in the first few weeks of school as they tried to assert their authority. Mr. Campbell's approach of blind trust was throwing everybody off.

As expected, the class separated according to cliques. Drew, Mila, and Anna lead the "fabulous" clique to the back left corner of the room. The hangers-on, Valerie and Jacey, soon followed. Andrew Wyatt, Charlie Mitchell, and Jake Allen, the star athletes, sat themselves directly across from the fabulous girls. Nettie, in an effort to avoid Drew Summers, moved as far away as possible to the front right corner of the classroom. Elisa found an empty seat next to her. The rest of the class filed in accordingly. Nerds to the front, wannabes in the middle, cool kids to the back.

When all seats were filled, Mr. Campbell asked, "Everyone situated? Good. As I said, enjoy these seats now. They will be yours for the next four weeks. Something tells me you'll all be disappointed with my seating assignments for the rest of the year, but I wanted to make sure we got off on the right foot."

Ah, the catch. Nettie secretly smiled. She always got a little kick out of watching teachers outsmart the cool kids. It was bad enough watching them control the schoolyard; she didn't need them feeling like they controlled the classroom as well. Nettie had to feel safe somewhere.

"As I mentioned before," Mr. Campbell continued, "this year we will explore our personal spirituality. This is not exclusive to just our belief in God. Personal spirituality requires delving into our own moral code. Who are you? What is your opinion? How do you feel? These are the types of questions I'll be asking and you will be expected to answer." Nervously, the students shifted in their seats. "Don't panic. I'm not going to invite Dr. Phil in here to moderate a roundtable discussion. What I mean is that I'm going to be asking you to keep a journal."

Several students moaned. "Now wait. I want you to give this a chance. I think you'll find by the end of the year that this will have been a very rewarding experience. What I'm going to do is give you topics, or prompts, if you will. On occasion, you'll be able to write anything you like. A freewrite we'll call it."

As he said this, he retrieved a stack of black-and-white speckled composition books. "These are your journals. Write your name on the front cover. I want to assure you that these journals are for your eyes only. I will not be sharing this information with anyone, not the school, not your parents, not your classmates. I will only be checking that they are completed, not reading them in great detail. I want this to be a free and safe medium for you to express your opinions and beliefs."

"Our first topic is this." Mr. Campbell went to the board and wrote "Who am I?" in chalk. "I want you to consider this question carefully before you write. This question is not as easy as it seems. You have ten minutes and your time begins now."

Nettie and her fellow classmates opened their journals and poised their pens, ready for the task at hand. Across the top of the first page of the journal Nettie wrote:

Who am I?

Nettie stared at the blank page. Mr. Campbell was right. This was not an easy question to answer. *Who am I?* Nettie considered her answer. There was the basic information. Nettie LuAnn Gaines, thirteen years old. Blonde hair, hazel eyes, average height, slim build. Smart. Okay, very smart. Somehow Nettie knew these were not the answers Mr. Campbell was looking for. *Then again*, Nettie wondered, *was there a right answer?* It was difficult to gauge Mr. Campbell on the first day of school. She had no idea what type of answer he was looking for. She wanted to believe what he said, that this journal was a safe zone and that her answers would not be judged. But Mr. Campbell was a teacher after all, and wasn't it his job to judge their work?

Before she drove herself completely crazy overanalyzing the situation, Nettie put pen to paper:

* * * *

August 30

Mr. Campbell says we have to keep a journal of our
eighth grade year. He says this will be a rewarding and
spiritual journey. We'll see. Our first task is to answer
the question, Who am I?

Who am I? I am obviously Nettie LuAnn Gaines. God I hate that name. I've never really told anyone how much I hate it, but I really do. I'm named after my great-grandmother on my mother's side. G.G., as we called her, was a famous singer in her time. She was called the "Soul of the Bay." I am honored to be named after her; she was an amazing woman. I just wish she'd had a better name. Nettie is so old-fashioned sounding. It's also plain and easy to make fun of. I cannot even begin to write all the ways my name is twisted into something insulting. But believe me, there's a lot of them.

I'm thirteen years old. I am smart. Very smart. I'm not trying to brag. It's not something I can help. It's just who I am. I was reading by age four and have never gotten a grade lower than an A-. I get made fun of for being smart. But like I said I can't do anything about it; it's who I am.

I don't have a lot of friends, but I have one good friend, Elisa Evans. Truthfully, I don't need more than her. I do not wish to be popular and have tons of girls clamoring for my attention. (I do not, no matter how often she says it, want to be like Drew Summers.) I do wish, however, that I were still friends with Andrew Wyatt. He and I used to be really good friends, before. Before he started going out with Drew. Before my brother Joe died.

I've never really thought about it before, but I am a girl who's suffered—a lot. My brother died in a car accident one week after his sixteenth birthday. My dad bought him a sports car, which my mother hated. They fought constantly about that car, both before and after Joe died. My father left the next year. And my friend, Andrew, the boy whom I thought I might someday marry, just stopped talking to me. To him, I am a geek. I am unpopular and apparently not worthy of his time. I wish this wasn't part of who I am, but it is.

I used to sing. Every chance he got, Joe would make me sing to him. We used to sing in the car together.

Joe was terrible at it, which always made me laugh. I inherited G.G.'s talent.

Joe made me promise to sing at his wedding and his funeral. I tried to keep my promise, but it didn't exactly turn out well. That's kind of a recurring theme in my life; things not working out the way I plan. I really wish I could change that about me.

Another part of me that I would like to change is that I am a tad on the unfortunate side. I'm a bit clumsy, and embarrassing things tend to happen to me. Like this one time in the sixth grade, I was reading to kindergartners in the library, and I let Johnny Redding sit on my lap, and he peed all over me. (And that's actually one of my least embarrassing moments.)

I guess if I had to try and answer the question in one sentence I would write: I am Nettie Gaines, the girl who all teachers leave in charge of the classroom when they leave, and the girl most likely to have toilet paper stuck to the bottom of her shoe.

CHAPTER FOUR
THE GOOD OLD DAYS

*T*he Wyatt's backyard looked something like a Norman Rockwell painting. The trees bloomed with bright green, waxy leaves and tiny cherry blossoms. The flower garden was in full bloom as well—roses, peonies and tulips. The grass, freshly mowed, made the perfect place to relax and enjoy the afternoon.

Nettie's father, Dan Gaines, and Steve Wyatt, Andrew's father, stood over the barbeque, arguing. Dan made several attempts to light it to no avail. He removed his Duke University baseball cap and wiped his brow. He replaced the cap and reached for his glass of lemonade. After a generous gulping, he lit a match and tossed it onto the coals. Nothing happened. Steve Wyatt raised his eyebrows at his friend and laughed.

"Joe! Grab some more matches from the kitchen!" Dan yelled.

"Dan, I'm telling you, you need to spread out the charcoals and not stack them up in a pyramid. That's why the thing won't light." Steve pointed at the barbeque.

"Relax, Steve. I've got it." Dan smiled reassuringly as he patted his longtime friend on the shoulder.

Under the apple tree, Andrew and Nettie sat and watched in amusement as their fathers continued to bicker for several minutes. Every time there was a barbeque, their fathers had this same fight. In the end, as always, Joe came over and lit the barbeque for them.

The clear blue sky stretched endlessly above them. It was hot, but under the shade of the apple tree it felt ten degrees cooler. Nettie lay on her back and looked up into the tree. "I hope the pie turns out okay," Nettie said as she sat up. "It's the first one I've ever made."

"My mom's probably got a frozen one in the freezer just in case."

"Thanks a lot." Nettie tossed a few strands of picked grass at Andrew. "I heard your dad tell my dad you're going to football camp. The one Joe goes to?"

"Yeah. I'm gonna be in Joe's cabin." Andrew fussed with his hair, brushing it off his forehead.

"It sucks that you'll be gone for such a long time. I mean you and Joe. You guys will be off having fun and I'm just stuck here," she said as she continued to pick grass. She bit the inside of her cheek, waiting for a response. She knew she would miss Joe terribly, as she did every year, but this year she would miss Andrew as well.

For as long as Nettie could remember, she'd spent her summers with Andrew. They'd spend the mornings riding their bikes or going on walks. They'd play hide-and-seek in Andrew's enormous house. When the weather was warm, they'd have water balloon fights. Nettie loved the summer for all those reasons, but mostly because she got Andrew all to herself. That was the way it was with summers, friends scattered to the four corners. But Nettie and Andrew, because they lived so close, and because their families were so connected, always had each other. She was not looking forward to their first summer apart.

"It's not that long. Three weeks." Andrew shrugged. "I've been waiting to go to this camp forever and now that I'm ten I can finally go."

"I know. I'll just be bored. And I hate when things change. I like things how they are now. What am I going to do when you guys aren't around?" Nettie pouted.

"My mom says she's going to write to me. You could do that too." Andrew shrugged again. "If you want."

"Will you write me back?" Nettie asked, sliding her glasses up the bridge of her nose. Andrew nodded.

"Really?"

Andrew looked right at her when he said, "Really. I'm ... you know," he flicked his hair again, "gonna miss you too."

Nettie lunged at Andrew and hugged him with all her might just as Joe walked over. "Hey, hey, lovebirds, there'll be none of that."

Nettie and Andrew quickly jumped back from the embrace. "We're not lovebirds!" Nettie snapped back. She knew Joe was teasing, but she wished he wouldn't embarrass her like that. Nettie didn't want Andrew to know how much she really liked him. What if he didn't like her back? For now, it didn't matter to Nettie that Andrew thought of her as nothing more than *just a pal. She didn't care what he thought of her really, as long as they were friends. She secretly hoped that one day, when they were old enough, Andrew would be her boyfriend. But she kept that wish to herself. She could wait. She could be patient.*

"Only kidding, Nettie. Take it easy." Joe looked Andrew up and down, folded his arms across his chest, and stuck his chin in the air. "So, what exactly are your intentions with Nettie?" Joe did his best impression of Dan Gaines, puffing up his chest and deepening his voice.

"Cut it out Joe!" Nettie yelled.

"Relax. Andrew knows I'm only messing with him." Joe leaned down and ruffled Andrew's hair.

"Hey stop that." Andrew tried to swat Joe's hands away.

"Sorry, am I messing up your hair?" Joe asked, mockingly.

"Stop!" Andrew continued to flail as Joe held him off.

"Come on pretty boy. What'cha gonna do about it?" Joe teased.

"Leave him alone Joe!" Nettie yelled.

Joe stopped and looked at Andrew. "Hey, if you're going to survive football camp, you're going to have to toughen up a bit."

"I'm tough," Andrew said defensively. He straightened his posture, trying to make himself taller.

"Well, come on tough guy. Show me." Joe motioned toward Andrew, egging him on. Nettie knew what came next. She'd seen them do this exact same little dance about a hundred times. She knew how it was going to end. She also knew that Andrew worshipped Joe and that he would do anything to win his favor. Nettie knew how Andrew felt. Joe was her hero too.

Joe leaned down into a three point stance, legs slightly more than shoulder width apart, hunched over at the waist with one hand, knuckles curled under, touching the ground. Andrew followed. Joe counted off like a quarterback. When he yelled hike, Andrew lunged for him like a pouncing tiger. Joe's swift movements seemed effortless as he stutter-stepped a few times and blew past Andrew toward the imaginary goal line. Andrew leapt at Joe, missed him entirely, and landed facedown in the grass.

Joe yelled over his shoulder, "I think you touched a little bit of my shirt that time," which was entirely untrue. He trotted back toward Andrew. The thing about Joe was that even when he was destroying you at a sport, you still loved him. He was all class and sportsmanship.

Andrew got up and dusted himself off. Joe wrapped him into a playful headlock. "One of these days you're gonna get me, kid. I just know it." They strode toward the house together with Joe's arm wrapped around Andrew's shoulders.

"Boys." Nettie rolled her eyes and followed them into the house.

* * * *

"Nettie! Nettie! Earth to Nettie!" Elisa shook Nettie's shoulder. "What were you thinking about?"

"Nothing. Why?"

"I've been trying to get your attention for like five minutes. The bell rang. It's time to go to lunch."

Nettie looked around the gym, a little disoriented. She had been watching her classmates play a rousing game of kickball when her mind wandered. She hadn't thought about that day at the Wyatt's in so long. She'd let herself get lost in the memory as if she were reliving it. Snapping back to reality, Nettie realized she was sitting in an almost empty gymnasium. Just Nettie, Elisa, and the equipment manager remained. As Nettie rose from the floor, Andrew emerged from the boy's bathroom. Standing face-to-face, Nettie and Andrew were momentarily frozen. Nettie thought for a moment that he might say something. Suddenly the bathroom door burst open, slamming hard against the wall. Charlie Mitchell and Jake Allen came barreling through.

"Andrew, let's go. The cafeteria is calling my name." Nettie watched as Charlie Mitchell eyed her from head to toe.

"Hey Nutty. Looking good in those gym shorts." Nettie blushed at the thought of her skinny legs protruding like chopsticks from beneath her baggy gym clothes.

"Shut up, Charlie." Elisa immediately came to her defense.

"Back off, Tree," Charlie laughed. Making fun of Elisa's obvious height advantage was his only defense. Nettie knew that if she wanted, Elisa could pummel him.

"Grow up, Sprout," Elisa snapped back.

Nettie snuck another glance at Andrew at the same time he looked at her. She thought about smiling, about saying hi to her old friend, but her lips felt glued shut. "Come on Elisa, let's go," was all she said.

Nettie and Elisa left the gym, leaving the three boys behind in their wake. When they were about twenty or thirty paces away they heard the boys erupt in laughter. Nettie silently prayed that she had nothing stuck to her behind.

Chapter Five

The Idea

The cafeteria smelled like fish sticks and tater tots, the Friday special. Students sat, eating and talking in various levels of rowdiness. A rogue spit wad flew in the direction of the lunch lady, Judy.

Nettie and Elisa sat together in the back right corner. The table, dubbed "The L Zone," by Drew Summers and her flock, was home to all those with above average grades. "The L Zone," despite being named "L" for loser, gave Nettie an interesting vantage point. From there the entire cafeteria lay before her. No one could sneak up behind her, leaving signs on her back or filling her backpack with soda. Nettie enjoyed this advantage and not just because she felt protected from pranks. From her comfortable seat, she could watch Andrew and Drew without being too obvious.

She couldn't help but watch them. Although most of the time it felt like pure torture. She hated the way Drew hung all over Andrew, draping her arm around his shoulder, playfully slapping his stomach. It was the only time Nettie ever felt jealous of anyone. She envied the way Andrew looked at Drew. It made her practically turn green thinking of how they talked, shared secrets, and kissed. They were a couple. They were close. And Nettie couldn't help but wish that it were she with Andrew, not Drew.

Beyond feeling jealous, Nettie felt disappointment. She was disappointed that Andrew would even choose someone like Drew. Drew was snotty, spoiled, and mean, nothing like Andrew. Or at least not the Andrew Nettie remembered. The Andrew Nettie remembered was sensitive, sweet, and caring. She tried and tried to think of all the things Andrew might like about Drew, but she struggled to come up with answers. All Nettie could think was that maybe there was more to Drew than she thought. Maybe when she and Andrew were alone together Drew turned into this really kind, warmhearted person. It was very possible that there was more to Drew than anyone knew. There was certainly more to Nettie than anyone cared to notice.

Drew ran her fingers through Andrew's hair and smiled wickedly at Nettie. *Nope,* Nettie thought, *she's just pure evil.*

The truth was Nettie didn't know Andrew anymore. She only knew the boy he'd been when they were young. He hardly resembled that boy now. When they were young, Andrew was a friend, someone she could count on. But now Andrew was just like all the other jerks in her class. He hung out with Charlie Mitchell and Jake Allen, the two guys most likely to get called to the principal's office. Nettie shook her head in disgust remembering the day last year when the three of them had received five hours of detention for putting Mentos candy into a Diet Coke bottle, which promptly erupted in a five-foot fountain all over the lunch room.

"What time is it?" Nettie asked Elisa. She had barely touched her tray of food, preferring reading to the risk of food poisoning from under-cooked fish sticks.

"Twelve ten. Why?" Elisa slurped the last drop of her Snapple.

"I just want this day to be over already." Nettie laid her head down on the table.

"Only a few hours left." Elisa patted Nettie's head. "What are we doing this weekend?" Elisa asked, just as Drew Summers and her pack of friends strode past their table on their way out to the schoolyard.

"As if you two have any real plans," Drew hissed.

"They might, Drew," Anna Winchester piped in, "maybe the library is getting a new shipment." The group giggled and high-fived each other before continuing past them.

"God, I hate them." Nettie stabbed at her fish sticks with her fork. "Why can't they just leave us alone?"

Elisa grabbed the fork from Nettie's hand. "Because it makes them feel better to make us feel worse."

"What does Andrew see in her anyway?" Nettie asked.

"Don't let her get to you." Elisa's red hair fell over her face as she leaned to the floor to retrieve her dropped napkin. Nettie envied Elisa's red hair. It cascaded and flowed, seemingly hypnotizing every boy who looked at her. Someday, Nettie hoped a certain boy would look at her the same way.

Nettie adjusted her glasses and tightened her ponytail. "I try. I really do. Just once, though, I would really like to get through the day without being reminded that he's with her. And did you see what Drew was wearing?"

"No. What?"

"She's wearing Andrew's watch." Nettie exhaled with great defeat in her voice.

"How fifth grade." Elisa rolled her eyes.

"I can't believe he gave her his watch." Nettie buried her face in her hands. "I thought for sure they'd be breaking up soon. My God, they've been together since last year. Aren't they sick of each other yet? We're only thirteen for crying out loud." As Nettie gestured wildly, her left arm knocked her milk carton over. The white river gushed and flowed down the table.

"Hey! Watch it!" the boy next to her yelled as he slid his tray away as quickly as possible.

Nettie's face grew red with embarrassment. She looked quickly to Andrew's table to see if he saw her spill. He had. Charlie Mitchell and Jake Allen were howling with laughter. Andrew looked away. *Of course.*

Elisa mopped up the spill as best she could with napkins. "Can't you just try and forget about Andrew? What about Justin Shay? He's cute. Why can't you like him?" Elisa asked, as if choosing someone to like was as simple as picking a movie to watch.

"You like Justin."

"I know, but who cares? We can like him together."

"Be serious," Nettie said. "Besides, I don't *really* like Andrew."

Elisa tilted her head and narrowed her eyes.

Nettie knew lying to her best friend was impossible. "Fine. I do. But what really kills me is how we were friends for years and now nothing. Now all of a sudden he's some big hot shot and I'm not worthy of his time." Nettie's shoulders slumped. "We used to talk, climb trees, hang out."

"You were ten." The thing about a friend, a real best friend, is that they know when to let you whine, but they also know how to keep you grounded in reality. No one was better at this than Elisa.

"I know we were ten, Elisa. But that doesn't mean his friendship didn't mean anything to me."

"I know. I'm sorry. Come on, the bell is going to ring." Elisa scooted her chair back and rose to her feet. Nettie followed.

With the sound of the bell, Nettie and Elisa headed to their lockers. Drew, Mila, and Anna were huddled together like a flock of sheep near the classroom door whispering. Nettie did her best to pretend she wasn't listening.

"I think we should do Andrew's next," Anna whispered. She ran her fingers through her chestnut brown hair and tucked a loose strand behind her ear.

"Not yet!" Drew yelled a bit too loud. She regained her composure and added, "We have to wait until he does mine."

"You could do his first. It would be great. We can all spend the night at my house tonight. My mom and dad are going to some charity thing at the club. They'll never notice if we leave," Mila offered.

"Mila, no!" Drew practically shouted. Their attempts to keep their conversation private quickly deteriorated as dozens of heads whipped around to see what the commotion was. "No girl ever does her boyfriend's house first." She looked toward Nettie before adding, "I'm not desperate or anything. Besides, he's going to do my house soon. I know it. And we'll wait until then." As the leader of the group, Drew always had the last word.

"So whose house are we doing then?" Anna asked.

Drew opened her compact and applied a fresh coat of peach lip gloss and said, "Charlie's."

Anna's eyes grew wide with horror. "No way!"

"Why not?" Drew snapped the compact shut. She glared at Anna, daring her to answer.

"Because we're not even together."

Nettie watched as Anna blushed. *How cruel*, Nettie thought, *to have a best friend like Drew*. For a moment she almost felt sorry for Anna.

"So?" Drew put her hands on her hip.

"Drew, you just said that the girl is supposed to wait for the guy to toilet paper her house," Anna reminded her.

For years, toilet papering houses had been a tradition at St. Elizabeth's. It was a way for the eighth grade boys to secure their date for the end of the year Grad Dance and to tell a girl they liked her without actually having to say it. No one knew when or why the tradition started. It seemed, to Nettie, like a strange and destructive thing to do. But she would be lying if she said she didn't fantasize about waking up one morning with her lawn decorated in two-ply streamers.

"You *want* to be together with Charlie, and this is the way to get him. You can't just sit back and wait for Charlie to do it. Charlie hasn't had an original thought in like five years." Drew rolled her eyes at Anna's hurt expression. "Come on. It's a great idea. This will get Charlie to notice you and by Monday he'll be asking you out. Just watch." Drew caught Nettie watching her. Nettie tried to avert her eyes, but it was too late. Drew was walking toward her.

"Can we help you with something?" Drew asked in her snottiest voice.

"No," Elisa snapped back. It amazed Nettie how unafraid Elisa was of Drew. The truth was Drew never confronted Elisa, never made fun of her because they were teammates. Although Drew most likely despised Elisa as much as she did Nettie, because they played volleyball together and Elisa was team captain, Drew never said a bad word to her on or off the court.

"Then stop staring at us," Anna said.

"Yeah, take a picture, it lasts longer," Mila added.

"We're having an A and B conversation here Nutty. Why don't you just C your way out of it?" Drew shooed them away with her hand.

"Wow I haven't heard someone say that since the fourth grade," Elisa sassed.

"We see you staring at us all the time, Nerdy. You, like, worship us or something," Anna said. Nettie hugged her books to her chest. She tried not to look at them. She tried to ignore them. All the pity she felt for Anna dissolved instantly.

Elisa came to her defense again. "Whatever," she said.

"I told Andrew you were like obsessed with me." Drew laughed. "He thought that was hilarious." Hatred oozed from her lips.

At the mention of Andrew's name, Nettie's face grew hot and red. She felt her hands begin to sweat and tears well up in her eyes. "You're such a witch, Drew," Nettie said through clenched teeth.

"Ouch." Drew pretended to sound hurt. The bell rang again signaling the beginning of the next class period. Drew and her group filtered into the classroom, their plaid skirts swishing in unison as they walked. Drew tossed her hair over her shoulder as she hissed, "I guess Andrew wants a girl who can do more than read."

Drew's parting words stung like a thousand bee stings hitting Nettie's heart. Nettie's blood boiled and her mind raced. She was sick and tired of Drew, of having to watch her and Andrew every day. She had to do something. Then it came to her, the perfect idea. Nettie turned to Elisa with a mischievous smile and said, "I just figured out what we're doing this weekend."

Chapter Six

The Great Toilet Paper War

"Elisa! Elisa!" Nettie tried to yell in her loudest whisper. She glanced back to make sure Elisa was following her. Even though they had ridden these same streets hundreds of times before, at night the roads seemed strange and unfamiliar. The trees seemed taller, more looming. A single bird chirp, a rustle of leaves sent chills up and down their spines.

They'd never done anything like this before, broken so many rules. They'd snuck out! They were supposed to be asleep in Nettie's room. They'd waited in silence for two hours until they were convinced that Nettie's mother was asleep and would not check on them. They slid out from under their covers, already fully-clothed. They'd grabbed their supplies and tiptoed down the stairs, avoiding the third one from the bottom, which creaked.

Once they reached the bottom of the stairs, they slithered on their bellies across the even creakier living room floor. At the kitchen they rose and carefully unlocked the back door. Then, because the door was swollen from the warm weather, they had to lift it slightly as they opened it so as not to arouse Nettie's mom. They knew she'd awake at even the slightest noise.

The trickiest part came in retrieving their bikes from the garage. *Why hadn't we thought to leave them outside?* Nettie silently cursed herself as she opened the garage door and stepped into blackness. Navigating without lights made the mission almost impossible, but she had no choice. If she turned on the light they were sunk for sure. As they made their way down the long driveway, walking their bicycles beside them, the motion censor light flicked on above them. They quickly huddled themselves next to the house trying not to move, even to breathe. When Nettie felt they were safe, she nodded to Elisa and again they made their way out into the cold, dark night.

"I'm coming!" Elisa barked back, her voice sounding unusually annoyed.

"You still want to do this, right?" With or without Elisa, Nettie was moving forward with their plan.

"Yes, I still want to do this."

They rode in silence until Nettie stopped at the corner of Bluegrass and Vine. They were only a block away now. "We're almost there. Don't back out on me now. This is going to be great. Now come on." Nettie and Elisa mounted their bikes and continued on to their destination.

The ride to Andrew's house felt longer than usual. He only lived a few blocks away, but the backpacks weighed them down. Elisa stopped twice to readjust her straps. Nettie did her best not to show her frustration. Nettie wasn't usually this impatient, but there was an urgency about tonight, an excitement Nettie had never quite felt before.

There was also something else to consider. They were not just sneaking out. They were in a sense challenging Drew. They were diving into a forbidden world, and if they were caught, there was going to be more hell to pay than any parent could possibly bestow upon them. According to junior high code, it was unheard of for "losers," as they were often labeled, to challenge the popular kids. Nettie knew full well that Drew would freak out and make her life more miserable than it already was if she ever found out. But for once, she didn't care.

Nettie stopped at the Dennison's house, four houses away from Andrew's. "Park your bike over here," she instructed. Nettie regularly babysat the Dennison twins, Marty and Maddy, the cutest six-year-old twins on the planet, so she knew they were not home. With the Dennison family away for the weekend, it was the perfect opportunity for them to safely hide their bikes in the driveway, sneak over to Andrew's house, and then sneak back.

They walked quickly and quietly the rest of the way to Andrew's house. The two-story, clapboard style house stood still and dark. Nettie took a quick look around for Andrew's cat, Sampson. If Sampson spotted them he'd be through the cat door and into the house meowing and hissing, waking the house better than any guard dog or alarm system.

Nettie unzipped her backpack, removed numerous rolls of toilet paper, and set them under the giant maple tree. Elisa set herself up across the yard next to Mr. Wyatt's lemon tree.

Standing across the yard, facing each other, Nettie and Elisa each took a deep breath. Then they both bent down and each took a roll of toilet paper.

"Ready?" Nettie whispered to Elisa. "One, two, three. Go." Nettie threw her roll as high as she could into the maple tree. The roll hit a branch, bounced off, and went hurtling back towards the ground. Elisa seemed to have a bit more luck as the toilet paper stuck to a branch on her first attempt. "It's working." Elisa smiled from ear to ear as she admired her first layer of paper in the tree.

"Keep going. We don't have much time." Nettie felt her heartbeat quicken. She threw the roll as high as she could, and this time it stuck. The paper clung to the tree like a giant wad of tinsel and then rolled down to the ground. Nettie grabbed her second, then her third roll, and continued with the same success. The tree was just about covered when she first heard the noise. It started as a small rustling sound, like wind through the trees, but as the noise grew closer it gained momentum. Nettie realized just in time what she was hearing. Footsteps!

"Someone's coming!" Nettie whispered as loudly as she could without being heard.

"Run!" Elisa dropped her last roll and ran off. They ran as fast as they could to the Dennison's house. They threw themselves onto the grass in the side yard, panting and gasping for air.

"That was close." Nettie's chest heaved up and down. She tried to catch her breath.

"I know. I thought we were dead for sure." Elisa finally relaxed and let out a little giggle. "Okay, that was way more fun than I thought it would be. I mean once the first roll stuck I got this burst of energy and then ..." She stopped mid sentence and her face turned white.

"What? What's wrong?" Nettie sat up and stared at Elisa, waiting for an answer, but all Elisa could do was shake her head back and forth.

"What are you looking at?"

It only took Nettie a moment to join Elisa in panic mode. Her backpack! She had left it behind.

"Your backpack! You left your backpack at Andrew's! We're caught for sure now!"

"Oh crap! Oh crap! We have to go back and get it." Nettie stood up and brushed off her jeans.

"No way!" Elisa shouted in horror. Nettie knew it was risky. They could get caught if they went back. But as she saw it, they had no choice.

"We have to. We can't just leave it there." Nettie looked to her best friend for support and found nothing. She knew at that moment she was going back alone. She straightened her jacket and stiffened her posture. "Fine. Wait here." Nettie took a deep breath to steady her nerves. She walked to the end of the driveway, turned left, and headed casually back to Andrew's house as if she were just another teenager out for a stroll at one in the morning.

As Nettie approached the house she could see that it was still dark. No lights were on, no sirens blaring. *So far so good.* Nettie saw her backpack lying next to the tree, right where she'd left it. But she also saw something she was not expecting. Sitting on the front steps, completely immersed in kissing, were Andrew's sister Jenna and her new boyfriend, George. Nettie dove onto the sidewalk, scraping her knee. Using the hedge that bordered the lawn for cover she lay there for a moment, motionless and terrified. *Come on Nettie, move!* Like a snake she slithered toward the backpack, looking up only once to peek at Jenna and George who had yet to come up for air.

Suddenly the porch light illuminated the yard. *Oh no.* The front door opened. Nettie froze. "Jenna? I thought I heard something out here." Mr. Wyatt checked his watch, "It's getting pretty late, don't you think?"

Jenna hopped to her feet. "I was just coming in." George, like Nettie, played possum.

"Yes, I'm sure you were."

Nettie peered through the bushes and kept her eyes locked on them. So far they had not noticed the toilet paper in the trees.

"Goodnight, George," Mr. Wyatt said. He arched his eyebrow at Jenna.

"Right." Jenna nodded toward her father. "Good night, George."

As George rose to leave and Jenna turned to step into the house, Mr. Wyatt did a visual sweep of the front yard. Satisfied, he too turned to go. He paused, foot almost in midair, and turned back around. Nettie's heart stopped. She knew it was over. "What in the world?" Mr. Wyatt walked down the steps, his neck craned towards the sky.

"What is it Dad?" Jenna asked. She followed his gaze to the trees and then she too saw it. "Oh my God. We've been TP'd!"

"How could you not see this?" Mr. Wyatt pointed to the toilet paper covered tree.

"Sorry Dad, I kind of had my mind on other things." She grinned in George's direction.

George took this as his cue to leave, "Good night Jenna, Mr. Wyatt." Nettie held her breath as George left through the yard. He was headed right for her! But instead of stepping on her he stopped and looked down at her backpack. "Hey!" George called to Jenna and Mr. Wyatt, "I found a backpack."

Kill me. Kill me right now.

George picked up the backpack and carried it over to Mr. Wyatt. Mr. Wyatt unzipped the main compartment and found nothing. He tried the small compartment and again found nothing. Nettie knew the backpack was empty. She silently thanked herself for removing all identification beforehand.

"Jenna, let's go on inside," Mr. Wyatt instructed, "there's nothing we can do about this now." Nettie only breathed again when she heard the door close behind them.

Luckily, George hopped over the side bushes and headed across the neighbor's yard and down the street without ever noticing the ball of terrified thirteen year old curled up on the sidewalk. Nettie picked herself up and trudged back to Elisa.

"What took you so long?" Elisa practically jumped on Nettie. "I thought something happened to you. I thought you got caught. I was just about to leave and go get your mother."

"Let's go home." Nettie walked over to her bike, picked it up, and peddled down the driveway.

"Wait! Aren't you going to tell me what happened?" Elisa peddled after her.

"Right now I just want to go home and crawl into bed."

"But Nettie, what happened to your backpack? Did anyone see you? Why couldn't you get it? Was it gone?" Elisa was not going to give up.

Nettie pulled up on the brakes, stopped, and turned around to face Elisa. "Don't you want to get out of here? I'll tell you everything when we get home."

"Hey!" A familiar, yet unexpected voice called out from the sidewalk.

"Oh my God," Nettie and Elisa said in unison. Andrew, in flannel pajama bottoms and a white undershirt, appeared before them. In his right hand he held Nettie's backpack.

"So it was you. I thought so." He glared at Nettie. Andrew looked angry and mean.

"I, um, we were just leaving," Nettie stammered. She could barely look at him.

He blocked her path. "Do you think this makes you cool? Do you think that throwing toilet paper on my house makes you part of our group? It doesn't. You're not my girlfriend, Nettie. You never were and you're never going to be." Andrew tossed Nettie's backpack at her feet.

Nettie stared at Andrew, at the boy she once knew. Somewhere inside was the Andrew she liked to remember. Nettie pictured him at the lake the summer they both went to Camp Hilmar. She could see them swimming together, eating ice cream together, and comforting each other when they felt homesick. They shared a flashlight on the night hike and they had even held hands when the counselor wasn't looking. Nettie remembered fondly the feel of his hand, hard and rough from playing football, rubbing against hers. It was the first time Nettie had held hands with anyone.

When Joe died, Andrew sat behind her at the funeral. Nettie could hear Andrew sniffling. She knew he was crying. She never turned around to look at him, but she knew. At the reception following the funeral, Andrew had been the one to find Nettie tucked in her closet with a flashlight reading *Tuck Everlasting*. He was a real friend back then.

Nettie thought of all this and began to cry. She tried to hold it in but the tears kept coming. Nettie had been teased plenty, called horrible names, been tripped in the hallway, or not told when she had toilet paper stuck to her shoe. But she had never quite felt the stabbing pain of being yelled at by Andrew.

She dropped her bike to the ground and marched right up to him. Andrew took a step back. "I hate you Andrew Wyatt. I hate you for being my friend and then acting like all of a sudden you're too good for me. And I don't want to be your girlfriend." Nettie threw her hands in the air. "God, you're so full of yourself!" She hung her head. And when she looked up there was a fire in her eyes. "Joe was wrong about you, Andrew. I wish he could see what kind of person you really are."

Nettie thought for a moment that Andrew wanted to say something. She watched him watch her. He looked hurt. Nettie hadn't expected to hurt him. She didn't think anything she said meant anything to him. She knew now she was wrong. She waited for him to yell at her, to say more mean things. But he didn't say anything. He just turned and walked away.

Nettie knew she'd crossed the line. No matter how angry she was at Andrew and no matter how badly he treated her, she knew she should never have mentioned Joe. Nettie reached down and picked up her bike. Without speaking a word to Elisa she peddled home.

After what felt like an eternity, they reached Nettie's house. They dropped their bikes on the lawn. Nettie slumped onto the porch. Elisa took a seat beside her. She put her arm around Nettie and said, "It's gonna be okay."

"No it's not," Nettie whispered. "Nothing is every going to be okay again." Nettie buried her face in her hands and cried.

"Yes it will. You and Andrew are just all messed up right now because of what happened with Joe. But come on, you know you guys are like destined for each other."

"What are you talking about?" Nettie wiped tears from her eyes.

"Don't act like you're all shocked. You guys have that whole Joey and Dawson thing going," Elisa said.

"Who are Joey and Dawson?" Nettie looked up confused.

"From that show, *Dawson's Creek*. My sister made me watch the DVDs with her. Anyway, there are two kids, Joey and Dawson. They grow up together and they are destined for each other. They'd break up, make up, and always find their way back to each other." Nettie looked up, feeling hopeful, and then Elisa added, "Of course, Joey ends up with Dawson's friend Pacey in the end, so this might not be the best example." Nettie rolled her eyes at Elisa.

Elisa recovered quickly. "What I mean to say is that no matter what is happening now, I really believe that you and Andrew have a special bond that no one, not even Drew Summers, can break."

"I used to think so." Nettie wiped her damp hands on her jeans, "But the truth is Andrew only ever really liked me when no one else was looking." Nettie hung her head with great defeat. It was how she truly felt and somehow saying it out loud made it real. Finally Nettie was beginning to accept another great loss in her life. First Joe, then her father, and now Andrew. It was official. All the men in her life were gone.

"Nettie, he does like you. I know he does. Even Drew knows he really likes you. Why else do you think she's so horrible to you all the time? She's totally threatened by you."

Nettie looked at her friend like she had just said the craziest thing in the whole world. "Elisa I know you're trying to make me feel better, but come on. Drew? Threatened by me? Yeah, right."

"Nettie, think about it."

"Think about what?"

"How did he know you were the one who TP'd his house? And how did he know where to find us?" Elisa asked. "I mean if he didn't care about you at all, how does he know so much about you?"

"It's not like it's a secret that I babysit the Dennison twins."

"I know. But he knows you well enough to know that that's where you'd be hiding." Elisa defended her position. "He knows you like no one else does, probably even better than I do. Because you guys are connected. Admit it."

"I'm tired and I'm going inside." Nettie rose from the step and went inside. She climbed partway up the stairs and froze at the sound of her mother's voice. Nettie thought she was caught for sure. She crept to her mother's bedroom to listen more closely. She heard her mother's voice, light and casual. *Is she on the phone?*

"Who is she talking to?" Elisa asked. "It's like two in the morning."

"Shh!" Nettie tried to listen through the door.

"Did she just giggle?" Elisa asked in a whisper. Again, Nettie shushed her.

Her mother was definitely giggling. Nettie thought she heard her mother say something about having a great time the other night. She racked her brain trying to think of where her mother had gone this week and why she wouldn't have told her.

* * * *

Freewrite

October 10

I can't stop thinking about that night at Andrew's house. Those things he said to me. He was so cruel, so heartless. I was pretty heartless too, I guess. I shouldn't have told him that Joe would be disappointed in how he turned out. That was low. But I was hurting. I still am hurting. It's not fair. None of this is fair. Why did I lose my brother, my dad, and my best friend? I don't understand why any of this happened to me. What did I do to make everyone leave me?

Right after my dad left, my mom made me see this counselor and she spent lots of time telling me that it wasn't my fault and I shouldn't feel responsible. She told me that life constantly changes and revolves and that we are sometimes helpless to it. She told me to learn to accept, learn to grieve, and learn to move forward. So far I don't think I'm having much luck.

I know that technically it's not my fault that my dad left, but I can't help wondering if maybe he didn't love me as much as he loved Joe. Why else would he just take off and leave me? Wasn't I a good enough daughter?

And it's the same thing with Andrew. He just stopped talking to me. I thought at first that maybe it was too painful to be at my house because of all the memories of Joe. But it's been three years and he treats me like I'm diseased or something. It's not right.

Something else is not right at home and I can't quite figure out what it is. When Elisa and I got home that night from Andrew's house, my mom was on the phone. She was laughing and saying how she had a great time the other night. I asked her about it and she told me she must've been talking in her sleep. I knew she was lying, but I didn't say anything. And now she's being mysterious. She's "worked late" twice this week. I know something's going on. So why won't she tell me? Is she dating? I don't really know how I feel about that. I guess I want her to be happy, but still, it's weird.

* * * *

35

CHAPTER SEVEN
THE LIBRARY

"Ah, we survived another week," Elisa exhaled as she removed a stack of books from the cart.

Friday afternoons, Elisa and Nettie worked in the school library, restocking the shelves. Nettie enjoyed the quiet of the library, and she felt at home amongst the books.

"I thought for sure this week would never end," Nettie sighed.

"That algebra test today was impossible."

"Uh-huh," Nettie muttered.

"Okay, not impossible for you, obviously."

"Sorry. If you want you can come over this weekend and I'll help you," Nettie offered.

"Thanks, but I have a volleyball tournament."

"Right." Nettie walked down the aisle and around the corner to the biography section.

"What are your plans?' Elisa asked, following her.

"Nothing."

"Hey, how come you don't take voice lessons anymore?"

"What?" Nettie was surprised by this question. She had not thought about singing in a very long time. "I don't know. I just stopped."

"But why?"

"I just stopped. It's no big deal." Nettie shrugged her off like the subject meant nothing to her. The truth was that she missed singing very much. But no matter how much she missed it, she wouldn't risk the humiliation of singing in front of anyone, except when she was singing along with the radio or a CD. And that was only because she could blend with the artist and not be recognized by those around her. She didn't want to talk about it with anyone either.

"Change of subject. My mom and I were supposed to go to a movie tomorrow, but last night she told me she thought she might have to work."

"On a Saturday? Wow, she's been working a lot lately."

"I know." Nettie placed the biography of Eleanor Roosevelt back on the shelf and pursed her lips, as if holding back words.

"What? I know that face. What's going on?"

"Nothing," Nettie lied.

"Come on. Spill." Nettie walked away to a nearby table and plopped down in a seat. Elisa seated herself across from Nettie and propped her head in her hands.

"Okay, but you have to swear not to tell anyone."

"Who would I tell?"

"Just promise."

"Okay, okay I promise."

"I think my mom is dating someone."

"Shut up!" Elisa yelled.

"Shh! Do you want Mrs. Clayton to come over here?" Nettie craned her neck to see if the librarian was roused by Elisa's little outburst. Luckily, she was nowhere to be seen.

"So do you really think she's seeing someone? Who? When? What do you know?"

"I don't know anything except that she's acting different. She's even dressing different. The other day she came home with shopping bags full of clothes."

"She could've just needed some new clothes," Elisa said.

"True, but then explain the late-night phone calls, the working late all the time."

"Maybe she's got a big case she's working on," Elisa offered.

"She'd tell me if that was it. We always talk about her cases, unless there's a gag order or something. I mean she doesn't violate attorney-client privilege or anything."

"Okay, I see your point. Why don't you just ask her?"

"I did. But I'm pretty sure she lied to me when she said she must've been talking in her sleep," Nettie answered.

"Seriously, if you're so concerned, just ask."

"I didn't say I was concerned."

"It's okay, Nettie. I'd be freaked out too if my mom started dating."

"My parents aren't even divorced yet."

"Really? I thought they were. When was the last time they spoke? Do you know?"

Nettie rarely liked to discuss her father's departure with anyone. She hated the questions, the looks of pity. Even though she knew Elisa meant well, it was no fun to have your best friend feel sorry for you.

"We haven't talked to my dad in two years." Nettie thought for a moment before adding, "At least I don't think so. I don't know anymore." She rose from the table and started pacing. "See, this is why this is driving me crazy. Why all the secrecy? What is she hiding? Is she talking to my dad again? Is that who she's dating?"

"Could be. I mean, maybe they're seeing each other secretly. You know to see if they can work things out before they involve you. They probably just don't want to get your hopes up before they know for sure."

Nettie stopped pacing and considered the idea. She liked it. And it did make sense. It would explain why her mother hadn't told her. It would explain the secrecy. Her mother was just trying to protect her.

"So, are you going to ask her?" Elisa asked.

"I don't know. Maybe I should just wait for them to come to me. I mean part of me really doesn't want to know unless it's for real. But could you imagine? Having my family back together? It would be amazing."

"It would be. I still think you should talk to her. It'll make you feel better to know for sure."

"You're right. I'll ask her tonight."

For the next hour and a half, Nettie stocked shelves with a mile-wide grin on her face. She pictured her family, together again, laughing, and healing. It would be a sad picture still, because Joe would not be there, but at least they'd have each other, like they should have all along.

CHAPTER EIGHT

HOPE FOR THE BEST, EXPECT THE WORST

Nettie paced back and forth in her room. She rehearsed opening lines like, "Mom, can I ask you something?" And, "Mom, what's new in your love life?" Nothing seemed right. Nettie never had trouble talking to her mother before. She always felt comfortable enough to ask her mother anything. So why was this so hard? Part of it was that her mother had not come to her first.

Nettie knew she should just march right into her mother's bedroom and ask, "Mom, are you dating Dad?" But what if they answer was no? What if her mother hadn't been dating at all? What if she was just working late? Or worse, what if she was dating, but just not her dad?

Nettie couldn't stand it anymore. She had to know.

She walked the short distance down the hall to her mother's room, pausing momentarily as she passed Joe's bedroom door. For three years that door had remained closed. Nettie thought for a second about moving on and how keeping Joe's door closed and never entering his room was probably the exact opposite of moving on. But she couldn't focus on that right now. Not when she had bigger issues at hand.

Nettie tapped lightly on her mother's bedroom door. "Mom?"

"Come in." Nettie entered the room and found her mother tucked under her covers watching a DVD of *You've Got Mail.* Her mother had a love of Meg Ryan movies that Nettie would never understand.

"Hi sweets. Want to watch the movie with me?" Annie asked, hopeful.

"Um. Sure," Nettie answered. She crawled into the bed next to her mother.

For a while Nettie watched the movie, blankly staring at the television screen. She tried to gather her strength. Finally, she spoke, "Mom, can I ask you something?"

"Of course. You can ask me anything."

"Is everything okay at work?"

"Everything is great. Why?"

"Well you've been working a lot lately and I was just wondering why."

"Oh, that. It's nothing, just some extra paperwork for a couple of cases," Annie answered quickly.

Nettie knew it was now or never. "Mom, are you dating someone?"

"What? Why would you ..." Annie paused. She took a deep breath and answered slowly, "You are too smart, kid. How did you know? I guess it doesn't really matter. Yes, I have been seeing someone."

Nettie's heart felt as though it might thump out of her chest. She'd been right. Her mother was dating. Now she just needed to know who her mother was seeing.

"Nettie, I hope you're okay with this," her mother continued, "I would've told you right away, but I didn't know how you'd react. And I couldn't risk upsetting you. We wanted to take things slow and see how things worked out before we involved you."

"So things are working out?" Nettie tried to conceal her excitement.

"Yes, things are going very well. I ..."

Nettie cut her mother off. "This is great, Mom, really great. Hey. I have an idea. Why don't you invite him for dinner tomorrow night? We can all have dinner, talk. Maybe watch a movie?"

"You really want to do that?"

"Absolutely. I just want you to be happy. And like you said, things are going really great. So why not!"

"Nettie I'm surprised you're taking this so well. I haven't even told you ..."

"You don't need to tell me any more. This is great. I'll help with dinner and everything. We can make pasta! We haven't done that in so long. I'll go to the store in the morning and get everything."

"Wow, Nettie, you are incredible. I am really impressed by your maturity."

"Thanks, Mom. I'm going to go make a shopping list. Good night." Nettie was out the door before Annie could answer.

CHAPTER NINE
THE DINNER GUEST

Saturday morning Nettie woke to an empty house. A note on the kitchen counter told her that her mother had gone to the office to pick up a few files. *Perfect,* Nettie thought, *now I can get everything ready.* Nettie grabbed the shopping list she'd made the night before. She double-checked it before heading out the door.

To get to the store Nettie had to pass Andrew's house. She deliberately walked on the opposite side of the street. Remnants of toilet paper remained in the trees. Nettie felt a small twinge of guilt at the idea of Andrew having to clean up the mess. But as soon as she remembered the things he said to her the guilt faded away.

The store was relatively empty for a Saturday morning. A few mothers struggled with loaded shopping carts and whiny children. Nettie waved to Mr. Green, the store manager, as she passed. Living in a small town all her life meant knowing many of the local business owners. It also meant that everyone knew about her brother dying and her father leaving. It took a long time before people stopping giving her "that poor girl" looks. Today Mr. Green simply smiled and waved hello.

Nettie stopped at the butcher counter first, ordering one pound of ground round and two pounds of mild Italian sausage. Next she stopped in the pasta aisle to pick up a box of penne. It was there that she came face-to-face with Andrew.

Nettie didn't know what to say. She wanted to turn and run, but that seemed childish. So she just stood there.

It was Andrew who spoke first. "Hey."

"Hi," Nettie said. She bit her inner lip.

"Shopping?"

"Yeah. You?"

"Just grabbing some stuff for Charlie's party tonight."

"Right." Nettie knew all about Charlie Mitchell's parties. The stories were well circulated by the following Monday. Most of the stories involved people making out in Charlie's pool house. Nettie cringed at the thought of Drew and Andrew kissing at the party.

"Well, I should go. My dad's waiting in the car."

"Okay." As Andrew turned to leave, Nettie took a step forward. "Andrew?"

"Yeah." He stopped and turned to face her.

"I'm sorry about the whole TP thing. It was a stupid thing to do."

"No big. My dad blamed Jenna's friends anyway."

"Oh. That's good I guess."

"Well anyway, see ya." With that Andrew turned and left.

Nettie returned to her shopping. She picked up the remaining items and began the short walk back to her house. She thought of her brief and odd conversation with Andrew the entire way home. She hated how awkward things were between them. She would have given anything to just talk to him again, really talk, like they used to. But she also knew that she should stop torturing herself. It was doing her no good to wish things would change. Andrew had a new life now. He was a star athlete. He had a gorgeous, albeit nasty, girlfriend. He went to parties that Nettie would never be invited to. She had to face the truth sooner or later. The Andrew she longed for no longer existed.

Nettie spent the next few hours in her room trying on different outfits. At first she put on her green corduroy skirt and a black sweater, but she felt too fancy. She didn't want to look like she was trying too hard. Nothing in her closet seemed to suit the occasion.

Her nerves were getting the better of her. After all, this was just her father coming to dinner. Sure it might be uncomfortable at first. But then they would talk and cry and laugh and be a family again. Of course part of her was still very angry that her father walked out, but the important thing was that he was finally coming home. In the end that's all that really mattered.

Finally, she settled on a pair of jeans and her favorite blue T-shirt. She threw her hair up into a ponytail and put on her black boots.

The afternoon was spent making pasta with her mother. They rolled meatballs and chatted, just like they used to. The house soon filled with the glorious smell of garlic and tomatoes. Nettie realized how much she missed that smell. Once the pasta was cooking and the garlic bread was in the oven, Nettie went up to her room to check her appearance one more time.

The doorbell rang at exactly six o'clock. She heard her mother open the front door. She crept out of her bedroom and tiptoed to the top of the stairs. She bent over the railing trying to catch a peek of her mother and father together again, but her mother was blocking her view. When he spoke, Nettie froze. He only said hello, but it was enough. *Oh no!* She tried to sneak back into her bedroom, but her mother called to her, "Nettie, come down, please. Our guest is here."

Nettie took the first brave step on the staircase. Her feet felt like lumps of dough, heavy and resistant to movement. Eventually, she made it downstairs and stood face-to-face with the dinner guest. She managed to say, "Hi, Mr. Campbell" when she reached the bottom.

"Hi, Nettie, how are you?" Mr. Campbell asked naturally. He looked nothing like the man she saw every day at school. His hair was unusually unkempt, wavy, and longer than she remembered. He looked clean-shaven, but there was a hint of stubble that gave him a more rugged look. His uniform of khakis, a button-down shirt, and necktie was replaced with black corduroys and a maroon V-neck sweater. He actually looked handsome. Well, as handsome as a teacher could be anyway. Nettie realized she was staring at him and that he'd asked her a question she hadn't answered.

"Oh, I'm okay. Thanks." Nettie passed them and walked into the kitchen. Her mother and Mr. Campbell exchanged looks. It was going to be a long night.

"Nettie, why don't you get Chris something to drink?" Annie asked, nudging her a little.

"Sure. What do you want?"

"Just water, thank you." Mr. Campbell gave Nettie a nice smile.

"Dinner is just about ready. Why don't you two go on into the dining room and I'll be right in," Annie suggested.

"Can I do anything to help?" Mr. Campbell asked. He seemed far too at home for Nettie's taste.

"No, I've got it." Annie smiled.

Nettie and Mr. Campbell walked into the dining room together. She sat down at her usual seat, and he looked at her as if he was unsure of where to sit. Nettie motioned toward the head of the table, where her father once sat.

Nettie tried to remember to breathe. Her mind was swirling; she felt dizzy. Her palms were clammy and she felt nauseated.

Mr. Campbell broke the silence. "So, this is pretty weird, huh?"

"I guess." Nettie shrugged. *Weird? This is way beyond weird.*

Annie appeared carrying the pasta bowl. Nettie had not noticed until now that she was wearing a new outfit. It was an emerald green wrap dress. It hugged her hips, showing off her curves. She wore heels, and not the low heels Nettie was used to seeing her wear for work. These were high heels, sexy heels.

Annie smiled widely as she said, "Dinner is served." She placed the bowl on the table and took her seat at the head of the table.

The conversation throughout the meal was sparse. Annie and Chris did their best to fill the air, asking questions, trying to get a discussion going. But Nettie was not taking the bait. It was as if her tongue had grown three sizes in her mouth and she was unable to speak. Occasionally she nodded or forced a smile. But no matter how hard she tried, words would not come.

Nettie's insides were churning. *How can this be happening? How could I have been wrong?* She wanted to slam her head against the table. She wanted to kick and scream like a three-year-old having a temper tantrum. This just wasn't right. Her mom could not be dating her teacher. This was just wrong. So very, very wrong.

Annie picked the napkin up from her lap and delicately dabbed at the corners of her mouth. She laid the napkin next to her plate and began to move her chair back from the table. "Well, anyone up for dessert?"

"No. I'm going upstairs." Nettie flew out of the dining room and up the stairs. She threw herself onto her bed and buried her face in her pillow. She wanted to scream. She hated feeling like this. Her skin crawled and her hands shook. If she could she would peel off her skin and disappear. She was tired of suffering, of having so many things in her life that were out of control.

It was another change, another curveball thrown at her, and she wasn't a good catcher. She had no mitt, no protective gear. Each pitch hurled at her hit her square in the chest and Nettie was sick of it. She wanted some control of her life. She wanted to be able to live without constant dread of the future.

A few moments passed before Nettie's mother appeared in her doorway. "Are you all right?" her mother asked.

"No." Nettie could hardly look at her mother. She tried to stay calm, but the anger she felt in the pit of her stomach would not stay settled. She rolled over and sat up. "How could you, Mom? My teacher? How did this happen? How long have you been seeing him anyway?" Nettie shouted.

"Please come downstairs and let Chris and I explain everything to you." Annie's voice was soft, loving. "Nettie, you seemed okay with this last night. I don't understand what changed. I understand it's a shock that I'm dating your teacher. But if you just give us a chance to explain, you'll see that everything is going to be fine." Annie reached for Nettie and instinctively Nettie wrapped her arms around her mother and let the hug envelope her.

"Mom, why would I ever think this is okay? He's my teacher. That's disgusting."

"But you seemed so fine with the idea of my dating someone."

"Yes, but that's because I thought ..." Nettie stopped. She couldn't continue. There was no way she could tell her mother what she'd really been thinking. How stupid she had been, thinking that her parents were going to just magically get back together.

"What honey, what did you think?" Annie asked.

"Nothing. It doesn't matter anyway." Nettie gave up. She gave up on her childish fantasy that her family would ever be whole again. Her shoulders slumped in surrender.

"Will you come back downstairs and talk to us?" Nettie flinched at the way her mother said "us." She was no longer referring to the "us" Nettie had known for the past two years. Now there was a new "us" in the picture. And Nettie worried about what that meant for her.

Together they walked back to the dining room.

Mr. Campbell smiled up at Annie and Nettie as they returned and took their seats at the table. "Okay, I know you have a lot of questions," Mr. Campbell started, "and your mom and I are here to answer all of them." Mr. Campbell and Annie exchanged looks.

Nettie wasted no time with her hard-hitting questions. "Are you even allowed to date my mom? I mean isn't it against school rules or something?"

"When we met I didn't know I was going to be your teacher. By the time we realized it, we liked each other too much to just give up." Mr. Campbell reached for Annie's hand, "And no, there's nothing in the school rules about my dating your mom. I talked about it with Principal Jacobs already."

Annie and Chris smiled at each other. Whether Nettie liked it or not, she knew by watching them that this wasn't going to go away anytime soon. But that didn't mean she was going to just accept it.

"You already talked to the principal! Great! Did everyone know before me?" Nettie was furious and she wanted to leave, to run, but she had to keep asking questions. She needed to know every detail. "Where did you guys meet?"

"We met at the movies." Mr. Campbell looked at Annie and smiled like he was remembering the night fondly. *Gross.*

"I'd gone to the movies while you spent the night at Elisa's," Annie chimed in. "The theater was really crowded, being a Friday night and all. Anyway, there was an empty seat next to me and Chris sat there. About halfway through the movie I went to put my soda cup back into the holder and I sneezed. I let go of the cup and spilled it all over Chris."

They laughed. Together.

"I felt so horrible. I kept apologizing. We were so loud the usher finally came and asked us to leave. We went to the lobby together and instead of being angry, Chris asked me if I'd like to get some coffee. We've been seeing each other ever since."

"So when was this?" Nettie tried to absorb all that was being told to her.

"July," Mr. Campbell answered.

Nettie felt her blood boil. "July? Are you kidding me? July! So you've just been hiding this from me this whole time?" Nettie swallowed hard and fought back the flood of tears accumulating behind her eyes.

Annie offered up an explanation, "Honestly, I didn't want to say anything to you until I knew how I felt about Chris. It wasn't worth it to me to upset you when I didn't know how things were going to work out between us."

"And now you know?" Nettie asked. Not only had they been dating behind her back for several moments, but now they were sitting before her as a united front. Against her.

"We felt it was time to tell you, yes," Mr. Campbell said. "Your mom and I care a great deal for each other. And we think it's time the three of us spend some time together."

Nettie felt a slight pang of sympathy for Mr. Campbell. He sounded sincere and kind and she could see why her mother liked him. She'd liked him too, until about an hour ago. But they were asking a lot of her and they knew it. The mature Nettie understood why they kept it a secret from her. She even sort of appreciated her mother's efforts to keep her from this painful moment for so long. The mature Nettie understood all of this. But the Nettie sitting at the table, watching them drool over each other, quite frankly didn't care.

"Nettie, are you all right?" Annie asked.

"Sure. Great. I think it's fabulous that you're dating my teacher," she said, her voice dripping with sarcasm. "Can I be excused now?" She looked to her mother for an answer and when she finally said, "Yes," Nettie hurriedly left the room.

* * * *

November 18

For the past few weeks I have been holding onto the biggest secret. My mom is dating Mr. Campbell. MY MOM IS DATING MR. CAMPBELL!!!!!!!!! I just can't believe it. Why would she do this to me? I know she didn't do this on purpose. I've listened for a while now to their explanations of how they didn't plan this and how they've tried to protect me—blah, blah, blah. But none of that matters. It doesn't change the fact that my mom is dating my teacher.

What was my mother thinking? I have to see this man every day, all day. It's killing me to just sit at my desk and act as if nothing is going on. What am I going to do?

I guess this means my parents are getting divorced. My mom and I haven't really talked about it, but I know it's coming. I just feel so stupid for actually believing that my dad was just going to show up at my house and we'd be a family again. I should've known better.

I haven't told Elisa yet. I don't know how to tell her. I know she'll be there for me, but I can't take any more pity from her.

I miss Joe. Every day I miss him a little bit more. I thought that over time it would be easier and I wouldn't miss him so much. But I need him. I need to talk to him. He would know what to do. He always knew exactly what to do …

* * * *

Parked in the driveway outside the Gaines' home was a 2003 convertible red Mustang with a huge red bow attached to the hood. Dan and Annie argued in the kitchen.

"Will you please just listen to me, Annie?" Dan pleaded.

"No! Why should I listen to you? It's not like you listen to me," Annie fired back.

"Be reasonable."

"Reasonable? Who are you to talk about reasonable? You just bought a $20,000 convertible for a sixteen-year-old boy!"

"Annie, please. Calm down. There's no need to get hysterical. We agreed to buy Joe a car. We agreed. You can't go back on that now."

"Give me a break, Dan. I did not agree to this! You knew how I felt about buying him a sports car. You knew and you just didn't care."

"Can't we just talk about this?" Dan approached his wife and tried to hug her. She backed away.

"Don't touch me!" Annie yelled.

At the top of the stairs sat Joe and Nettie. They looked worriedly at each other, but did not speak. Their parents had fought before, but never like this.

"Annie. I know you're upset, but Joe is a very responsible young man. He works hard and I know he can handle the responsibility," Dan said.

"I know that. Joe is very responsible. But this isn't just a car. This is a death trap."

"It's not a death trap. Joe will be perfectly safe. He's a good driver."

"It doesn't matter! I know he's more responsible than most boys at his age, but Dan, a sports car is too much. They are built for speed, for exhibition. It's not an appropriate choice for our son."

"You'd rather I'd given him a minivan?" Dan said sarcastically.

"That's great, Dan. Mock me. But if something happens to my son while driving this car I swear I'll never forgive you. And I'll never forgive myself for allowing this."

Joe rose from his perch on the stairs. He slowly walked toward the kitchen. "Mom," he said, "If you don't want me to have the car, we can take it back." Most newly-licensed sixteen-year-olds were probably not so reasonable. But Joe was. It was one of things Nettie admired most about him. He was unlike any other boy she knew. He was smart and sensible. To Nettie, Joe was perfect.

"Oh, baby." Annie cupped Joe's head in her hands. "It's not that I don't want you to have a car. I do. I'm just not comfortable with this car." She let go of Joe, turned to Dan, and yelled, "I don't appreciate your father going behind my back and buying you a sports car!"

"I did not go behind your back!" Dan shot back.

"Guys, stop yelling," Joe interrupted, "You're upsetting Nettie. It's no big deal. I'll just take the car back and get something else. Okay, Dad?"

"No, it's not okay. You're my son and this is my gift to you." Annie glared at him. Dan corrected himself, "Our gift to you. Your mother and I will work this out, I promise. Won't we, Annie?"

"I guess." Nettie heard the defeat in her mother's voice.

"See Joe, everything will be fine. Now, why don't we take this bad boy for a spin?" Dan removed a set of keys from his pocket and dangled them in front of Joe.

"Mom is this okay with you?" Joe asked.

"Does it matter?" Annie asked as she left the room. She ignored Nettie as she stomped past her on the stairs. Nettie looked over her shoulder at her mother just in time to see the bedroom door slam shut.

CHAPTER TEN

SONGBIRD

On a Tuesday afternoon during her free period, Nettie sat in an empty classroom grading papers for the second grade teacher, Mrs. Cleary. It was one of the joys of being responsible and trusted by teachers. Nettie looked over each spelling test, marking mistakes with a slash mark and drawing big red stars across the tops of papers without any errors. When she was finished, Nettie grabbed the bathroom pass off the wall and headed down the hall.

She closed the bathroom door behind her. She turned on the faucet and washed her hands. As she ran her hands under the facet, Nettie began to hum. She did it unconsciously at first, without realizing that she was humming one of her great-grandmother's songs. She sang a few bars, to see if she could remember all the words. She could. She sang the song, with the water still running to muffle the noise. It felt nice to sing again, like finding a favorite pair of missing shoes at the back of the closet.

Nettie thought about how much she used to love to sing and about that horrible day when she vowed never to sing again. She'd told her mother that she'd simply lost interest in singing. Soon after, the voice lessons were cancelled and eventually her mother relented and stopped pressuring her to pick it up again.

Lost in thought, and song, Nettie barely heard the knock on the bathroom door.

"This is Mr. Campbell," he said as he knocked on the door. "Come out here please."

Nettie turned off the water and went to face her teacher. "Mr. Campbell?"

"Nettie, who else is in the bathroom?"

"No one."

He looked puzzled. "I heard someone singing."

"Oh. You did?"

Mr. Campbell arched his eyebrow in suspicion. "Was it you?"

Without looking at him she whispered, "No."

"Then who was it?"

Nettie lifted her eyes and met Mr. Campbell's disappointed look head on. "I really don't know." She wasn't about to tell him it was her he heard singing in the bathroom.

"Then explain the music," Mr. Campbell demanded.

This she could not do. Was it really any of his business? Lots of people sang in the showers, Nettie sang while she washed her hands. She wasn't hurting anyone. She thought, obviously incorrectly, that she wasn't making that much noise.

Nettie lowered her head back to her shoes. "I can't."

"Nettie, I don't expect this kind of behavior from you. Something is going on and I want to know what it is right now. Explain yourself."

Nettie thought of all the excuses she could give him, like she heard the noise too and wondered where it was coming from, but that sounded stupid. Quickly she blurted out, "I had a radio."

Mr. Campbell looked at her for a long time. Nettie wondered what he must be thinking and whether or not he would believe that Nettie, the most responsible girl in eighth grade, would blatantly break a rule.

He sighed loudly before he spoke, "Okay, I have no other choice then. I'm going to have to give you detention, after school in my classroom." Nettie nodded and walked past him down the hall.

Chapter Eleven

Detention Surprise

After the final bell rang all the students gathered up their belongings and headed off to their various destinations—football practice, soccer practice, piano lessons, home. Nettie headed off to detention. She cleared her locker of books she'd need for that night's homework, grabbed her sweater off the hook, and walked back to her classroom. She sat down at her desk and waited for the other students to arrive. At 3:25 she was still the only one in the classroom. *Maybe no one else got detention today.* Finally, Mr. Campbell appeared. He looked unusually chipper for someone about to oversee an hour of detention.

"So, here we are, Mrs. Morgan should be here momentarily." He said this as if it should mean something to Nettie, but it left her more confused than ever. Just as she was about to ask what was going on, Mrs. Morgan entered the room.

"Are we ready?" Mrs. Morgan asked. Mrs. Morgan, the drama and arts teacher at St. Elizabeth's, also led the choir at Sunday mass. She was a stout woman, potato shaped, with grayish blonde hair cropped in a neat chin length bob, beautiful chocolate brown eyes, and a warm smile. All the kids liked her.

"We're ready. Come on Nettie, let's go." Mrs. Morgan and Mr. Campbell turned to leave. Nettie followed behind. She realized right away they were headed for the music room.

Mrs. Morgan instructed Nettie to stand by the piano. "We should start with some warm-ups first," she said as she began to play scales on the piano. "Just follow me, Nettie." Then she sang the notes of the scale, making an "ah" sound.

"Wait, what's going on?" Nettie looked at Mr. Campbell for an explanation. Everything was happening so fast. Nettie's head was spinning. He knew! Obviously Mr. Campbell figured out it was her singing in the bathroom and now he wanted a private performance. Although Nettie was accustomed to humiliation, she'd never experienced being tricked by a teacher.

"You can do it," Mrs. Morgan reassured her, "just follow my voice." Mrs. Morgan played and sang again. This time Nettie followed. The notes came easily to her. Just as they always had. Nettie's voice felt open and clear. It felt great. She felt a rush, a surge of energy. She liked it.

It was Mrs. Morgan who'd been Nettie's singing teacher years ago. Nettie remembered fondly spending afternoons with the sweet woman, singing and laughing. Mrs. Morgan, a fan of Nettie's great-grandmother, knew all her songs on the piano by heart. Nettie hadn't thought of just how much she truly missed singing, and Mrs. Morgan, until now.

"Now that we're good and warmed up, shall we try a song?" Mrs. Morgan suggested.

"I guess." Nettie nodded.

Mrs. Morgan winked and said, "Let's try an old one." Her fingers moved nimbly, floating from key to key. As she played the familiar notes, Nettie's heart leapt. Nettie closed her eyes and before she could talk herself out of it, she was singing. She sang despite the fact that Mr. Campbell was staring at her.

For once Nettie didn't care. She wanted to be angry with her mother for telling Mr. Campbell that she could sing. She wanted to be angry with Mr. Campbell for setting her up, but she just couldn't. She didn't care that her secret was out. It felt so good to sing again. It felt good to connect to a part of herself that she had stifled for so long.

She felt slightly nervous about Mr. Campbell hearing her, but as the air filled with her voice, her fear subsided. By the time it was over, Nettie had forgotten he was even in the room.

When she stopped, Mr. Campbell and Mrs. Morgan enthusiastically applauded. Her cheeks reddened, uncomfortable at first with their jubilation. Her first instinct was to shrink away, but instead she let herself enjoy the moment. She let herself feel proud. And it felt really good.

"That was wonderful Nettie! You are amazing," Mr. Campbell gushed as he ran to congratulate her.

"Really, Nettie, you are very, very talented." Mrs. Morgan rose from the piano to give Nettie a hug. "You have a special gift, my dear. Nettie Lu would be proud."

The compliment was so overwhelming, Nettie wanted to cry. She finally managed to say, "Thank you."

Nettie looked at Mr. Campbell suspiciously. She wasn't going to just let him off the hook. She wanted confirmation that he knew she could sing. "You knew, didn't you?"

"Who, me?" Mr. Campbell's eyes widened as if totally shocked by her accusation.

"My mom told you, didn't she?" Nettie asked.

"Don't be angry with her. She just mentioned that it was something you used to enjoy."

"So why didn't you just tell me that you knew I was singing in the bathroom?"

"I wanted to hear you sing." He smiled. "So why don't you sing anymore?"

Nettie knew this was her chance to tell the truth. She could just tell him that she stood up to sing at Joe's funeral, froze, and practically fainted on the altar. She might as well tell him, before her mother did. But she just couldn't.

"I get stage fright."

"I see," was all Mr. Campbell said.

Nettie expected him to say more, to give her all the same cheesy lines she'd heard over the years about picturing the audience in their underwear or focusing on one spot against the back wall, but Mr. Campbell offered none of that. He simply said, "You're free to go."

Nettie was beginning to understand why her mother liked Mr. Campbell so much. He seemed pretty nice. Sure, he'd tricked her into singing, but the truth was, she loved it.

"Mr. Campbell," Nettie said, "Thanks."

CHAPTER TWELVE

DECK THE HALLS

Elisa and Nettie sat at opposite ends of Elisa's L-shaped couch. They wore comfy clothes and their favorite slippers. They snuggled beneath blankets. The Christmas tree, freshly decorated with angels, candy canes, and various ornaments, glowed with colorful blinking lights.

Nettie looked over the tree, thinking back to Christmases past. She remembered what her Christmas tree looked like before Joe died, before her family was torn apart. They went to the same tree farm every year. Joe always let Nettie pick the tree without argument. Nettie picked some weird looking trees over the years, but every time all Joe said was, "Nice choice, sis."

The coffee table had been transformed into a buffet of junk food—popcorn, Red Vines, M&M's—all the staples were represented. Every year, Elisa and Nettie gathered together to watch their favorite Christmas movies. They started with *Miracle on 34th Street,* followed by *A Christmas Story*, and then they paid tribute to Joe by watching his favorite Christmas movie, *Yogi's First Christmas.* It always made Nettie laugh thinking of Joe and his cartoons. Sure, lots of boys watched cartoons, but unlike most boys, Joe had a soft spot for *Yogi Bear, The Jetsons*, and *Super Friends.* Joe always used to say that the cartoons of the '80s were the best.

"I can't believe it's already Christmas again," Elisa began, "it feels like we just started eighth grade and now it's almost over."

"You sound like my mom. Oh my baby is getting so big." Nettie did her best impression of her mom.

"Shut up!" Elisa tossed a handful of popcorn at Nettie. "I'm serious. We're almost in high school."

"Crazy." Nettie reached for a handful of M&M's.

"What do you think high school will be like?" Elisa asked as she stuffed an entire Red Vine in her mouth.

"Don't know." Nettie wasn't ready to tell Elisa that just thinking about it terrified her. High school meant even more change in Nettie's life. Although she welcomed some of the change, like not having to be in the same classroom as Drew Summers all day long, most of the changes were too scary to think about. Would she make friends? Would she still be a nerd? Would she ever get asked to a dance? Would she ever be kissed? These thoughts swirled and swished around in Nettie's mind, making her dizzy.

"Do you think we'll get the same classes?" Elisa asked.

"Maybe." Nettie considered for a brief moment the idea of being alone, without Elisa by her side. She shuddered at the thought. "I hope so. At least we'll have the same lunch period, all freshmen do. So we'll be able to sit together," Nettie said as she munched her candy.

"True. You think Andrew and Drew will still be together?" Elisa asked.

"Elisa, I really don't want to talk about them tonight." Nettie picked up the remote control and pressed play, hoping to end the conversation.

"Sorry, just asking." Elisa threw up her hands in self-defense.

"Okay, change of subject. I have something to tell you. You have to swear not to tell anyone." Nettie looked seriously at Elisa. She pressed pause on the DVD player and turned to face her friend.

"Nettie, you know I won't," Elisa promised, crossing her heart.

"I know. I know. But this is big. Huge. Like the biggest secret in the history of secrets."

"What is it? I'm dying." Elisa begged and she bounced up and down on the couch.

Nettie opened her mouth, closed her eyes and said, "My mom is dating Mr. Campbell."

"Shut up!" Elisa squealed. "Seriously? You're kidding, right? Oh my God! Oh my God."

"Calm down. It's not that big a deal," Nettie said nonchalantly.

"Um, excuse me. It's freakin' huge!" Elisa said.

"Okay, I know it's huge. But try not to get hysterical."

"Tell me everything. Don't leave out any details." Elisa crossed her legs and sat up, giving Nettie her full attention.

"They met over the summer at the movies. She spilled her drink on him, they got to talking, and they've been dating ever since."

"Did you just flip out when she told you?" Elisa asked.

"Kind of. He came over for dinner."

"*When?* How could you not tell me that? Nettie!" Elisa scolded.

"I just couldn't. I didn't want anyone to know. But they all will soon enough."

Elisa looked curiously at Nettie. "Why?"

"Well, you know how my family used to throw New Year's parties?" Nettie asked and Elisa nodded. "We're throwing one this year. I mean, my mom and Chris are."

"Ew! You called him Chris!" Elisa flopped onto the couch and laughed.

"It slipped." Nettie shrugged. "I call him Chris when we're not in school. It took me a while to get used to it." Nettie threw a pillow at Elisa, hitting her in the face.

Elisa stopped giggling and her face grew very serious. "Wait. What about your dad?"

"Don't know." Nettie shrugged. "My mom said she talked to a lawyer about getting a divorce."

"Wow." Elisa tried to process all of this information. "How are you about all this? You seem so cool. I'd be a wreck."

"I was, at first. I guess I've gotten used to it." Nettie smiled, "Okay, I admit it's weird but he makes my mom really happy. She's not as lonely. I just hope that I still fit, you know?"

The truth was, Nettie was getting used to the idea of having Chris around. She'd almost forgotten what it was like to have a male presence in the house. She liked the different smells and tastes Mr. Campbell brought to the house. He brought flowers. Nettie had forgotten that flowers were meant to brighten a room, not just a headstone.

He liked popcorn and milk together, like cereal. At first Nettie thought it looked disgusting, but once she tried it, she really liked it. She liked lots about Mr. Campbell. Mostly she liked the way he made her mother laugh. That was not just a good thing; it was a great thing.

She did wonder, from time to time, how she fit into the new picture. What was Chris to her? He couldn't just be her teacher anymore. He couldn't be just her mother's boyfriend. She hadn't figured it all out just yet. She just hoped this new family that she was growing to love didn't leave her. It wasn't a ridiculous or irrational fear. It had happened to her before.

"Why wouldn't you fit in?" Elisa asked.

"What if they get married and start having babies? Where does that leave me? Since Joe died it's been just me and her. Now there's him and they are a 'they.' It's weird."

"Yeah, it will be weird when everyone finds out. I mean, can he even do that? You know, date your mom?"

"I guess so. It's not against school rules or anything. And I already get really good grades so it's not like anyone can accuse him of padding my report card."

"True. Still, it's freaky. Your mom's dating our teacher. I would die if my mom was dating my teacher."

"Luckily, your parents are still married," Nettie reminded her.

"True. Okay, as long as we're making big announcements, I've got one for you."

"Good. I'm tired of thinking about Mr. Campbell and my mom."

"Well, this will definitely take your mind off things."

"So is this good news or bad news?" Nettie asked while she reached for the M&M's.

"Oh, it's good news. Very good news." Elisa said with a mile-wide smile.

"Tell! Tell!" Nettie demanded.

"Justin Shay asked me out," Elisa gushed.

"What?" Nettie almost choked on her M&M's.

"Last week, after school." Elisa's cheeks were turning so red they almost matched her hair.

"That's so great! Why didn't you tell me?" Nettie was disappointed that her best friend hadn't shared such good news with her right away.

"I just didn't want to upset you. I mean with everything that happened with Andrew, I don't know. I should've told you. Sorry." Elisa got up to hug Nettie.

"So, you're going out with Justin." Nettie paused, taking a moment to fully let the news sink in. "Does anyone else know?"

"Um, not really. It's not like we're trying to hide it or anything. We're just keeping it low-key for now." Elisa pursed her lips together as if she had more to say.

"What?" Nettie asked.

"He asked me to the Grad Dance."

"The Grad Dance! That's five months away. He must really like you." Nettie was really happy for her friend, but she couldn't help feeling sorry for herself. She didn't have a date for the dance. And she knew that even if she was asked, it wouldn't be by Andrew, therefore, it wouldn't be the same.

"I know. I was so surprised." Elisa collapsed back into a mound of pillows and practically squealed as she said, "Oh, he is so cute. Don't you think?" Elisa's moon-eyed expression made Nettie laugh a little.

"Very cute. That's so great, Lis." The phone rang and Elisa jumped up to answer it. "Maybe that's him!" Nettie teased. Nettie could tell by the way Elisa smiled when she answered the phone that it was Justin. Alone in the living room, Nettie pressed play on the DVD. Watching the movie, Nettie realized that everyone around her was finding love.

* * * *

My Christmas Vacation

December 30

Christmas was great! It's been such a long time since Mom and I truly enjoyed Christmas. We hung Joe's stocking like we always do. It's kind of sad reminder. But it would feel worse not to hang it at all. We didn't hang Dad's this year. I guess it wouldn't be right. I mean he's the one who chose not to be part of our family anymore. So why should we care about his stocking?

Anyway, on Christmas morning we got up and opened presents. Mom gave me the usual, clothes and stuff. She gave me a gift certificate to the bookstore, which I will be using very soon. I gave her my school picture in a frame, like I always do, and I gave her a gold necklace with a heart pendant. I saved my babysitting money for months to buy it. She loved it and it made me beyond happy to see her smile like that. But she saved her biggest smiles for breakfast. That's when Chris arrived. He came loaded with gifts. I thought it would be weird at first, getting gifts from a teacher, but he's really becoming a friend. He gave me lots of books, some of them really old and dusty. I can't wait to start reading them. Chris gave my Mom some DVDs and a gold bracelet. It's really pretty.

We ate breakfast together and then Chris did the dishes. We watched movies and played a couple hands of poker. Chris is teaching me how to play and of course letting me beat him.

The best part of the day was dinner. Chris can cook. He made the most amazing turkey dinner! It was so nice to have him with us. It felt like a family, something we haven't felt in a really long time.

Tomorrow is the big party. I'm pretty excited about it. Andrew is coming. It will be just like old times, sort of.

CHAPTER THIRTEEN

SOME PARTY

The doorbell started ringing at seven thirty and continued to ring every few minutes for an hour or so. The Gaines' house was bustling with guests sipping champagne and laughing. Annie introduced all of her friends to her new boyfriend, Chris Campbell. Nettie watched as the guests greeted each other with friendly handshakes and warm hugs. It felt indescribably great to hear and see her house full of so much happiness. Nettie and Elisa took coats at the door and helped serve food. They loved listening to the adults catching little pieces of gossip here and there.

Nettie paced by the door waiting for Andrew and his family to arrive. When they finally did, Nettie couldn't get over how amazing Andrew looked. His blue shirt matched his eyes perfectly. Nettie was just about to tell him this when she noticed one very uninvited guest.

"Hi. Nettie. Andrew said you wouldn't mind if I came to the party. It's all right, isn't it?" Drew tossed her coat to Nettie as she walked past her. "Nice house."

Nettie looked to Andrew, waiting for some type of apology signal. He could nod or smile, give her the "I had no choice" look. But he didn't. He avoided Nettie altogether.

The Wyatt family entered the home and each, except Andrew, exchanged a hug with Nettie. Mr. Wyatt explained that Jenna had plans with George and couldn't make it. Nettie figured Jenna wouldn't come. She hadn't been back to the house since the funeral. As soon as the Wyatts were settled with drinks, Nettie and Elisa slipped away. They huddled together in the kitchen, whispering.

"Why would he bring her here?" Elisa asked, shocked.

"Probably because she's his girlfriend," Nettie replied flippantly.

"Still, it's rude. God he bugs me," Elisa said as she chomped on a carrot stick.

"Is Justin coming?" Nettie asked, desperate to talk about something else.

"Yeah, he should be here soon." With those words, Justin entered the kitchen. Justin stood almost six feet tall, huge for an eighth grader. He styled his dark brown hair into what looked like a field of tiny spikes. He had big brown eyes and a nice smile. He was handsome, not just cute. He looked much older than thirteen, with a strong jaw line and distinct features.

"Hey, I've been looking for you two," Justin said.

"Hi, Justin." Elisa's whole face lit up at the sight of him. He gave her a hug and a little peck on the cheek.

"What are you guys doing in here?" Justin asked, and then answered his own question. "I saw Andrew out there with Drew. That's gotta suck, huh?" Nettie looked stunned. *What had Elisa told him?*

"Whatever. I'm going to get something to drink." Nettie left the kitchen and headed for the temporary bar, which was set up in the dining room.

"What's wrong with her?" Justin asked. Elisa just rolled her eyes at him.

The party raged on for hours, with midnight approaching fast. Nettie spent most of the night trying to avoid Andrew and Drew on one end of the house and Elisa and Justin on the other. It was hard to be a lone fish in a sea of couples. Finally, she gave up walking in circles and stayed in her room reading one of the books Mr. Campbell had given to her for Christmas.

Unexpectedly, the bedroom door flew open. "Whoops! Thought this was the bathroom," Drew said scanning the room. She scrunched her face as if she'd smelled something horrid and said, "Well, I guess I was close."

"It's down the hall," Nettie said without looking at Drew.

"My God, Nosey, there's a party going on downstairs and you still can't manage to tear yourself away from your precious books." Drew continued to inspect Nettie's room, making little faces here and there. She picked up a picture frame holding a photo of Nettie and Andrew when they were young.

Nettie walked over and took it out of her hands. "Can I help you with something, Drew?"

Drew looked Nettie up and down. "Actually, I was thinking maybe I could help you."

"Like I'd ever want your help with anything," Nettie said defensively. She put the picture in a drawer.

"I'm serious. Look, you're not completely hopeless. You're okay-looking and you're smart. You could be one of us, you know," she paused, "your brother was."

Nettie stiffened at the mentioning of her brother. "You didn't know my brother."

"I mean you could be popular, part of our crowd." Drew eyed Nettie's outfit. "If you tried."

"Drew, this may come as a shock to you, but I don't want to be part of your crowd." Nettie stood by her door letting Drew know she wanted her to leave.

"Maybe not. But you want Andrew." Nettie's throat closed and her heart pounded. Drew's head cocked to one side and her eyes narrowed. "Don't you?"

"I do not!" Nettie yelled.

"Whatever. But you should know that it's not cool to like someone else's boyfriend." Drew picked up a teddy bear from the corner chair, "I mean, I don't know how you do things in Geek Land," she said as she eyed Nettie's unicorn posters, "but in my world liking someone else's boyfriend is really low."

Nettie's anger grew and steeped like a kettle about to boil. This was her room, her space, and she was not going to let Drew intimidate her in her own house. "For the last time, I don't like Andrew. And I'd rather live in Geek Land then have to be friends with you." Nettie grabbed the teddy bear out of Drew's hands. "Now if you'll please leave, I'm reading." Nettie gave Drew a light shove toward the door.

"I'm going. I'm going." She paused, turned around and took a couple of steps back into the room. "You know, Nettie, it really is sad that your brother died." Drew picked up another frame, this one holding Joe's football portrait. "He was so gorgeous and popular." She paused, looked at Nettie, and laughed. "So unlike you."

"Get out!" Nettie yelled as she yanked the picture from Drew's hands.

"With pleasure. I shouldn't keep Andrew waiting anyway. It's almost midnight and I know he's just dying to kiss me." Drew finally left the room. Nettie slammed the door behind her.

CHAPTER FOURTEEN

SNEAKY SNEAKY

With winter break over, life returned back to normal. Nettie spent most of her time trying to forget about her nasty run-in with Drew. The first few days back at school Nettie had managed to avoid any interaction with Drew and her crowd. Word spread quickly about Nettie's New Year's Eve party and Mrs. Gaines' new boyfriend. Surprisingly, the fallout hadn't been as horrible as Nettie expected. A few whispers, a few laughs, all the stuff she was used to; it hardly bothered her. She actually felt like she'd dodged a huge bullet. Maybe her luck was changing. Maybe she wasn't cursed after all.

Nettie sat at her desk writing in her journal. Mr. Campbell typed on his computer, his keystrokes fast and intentional. Every once in a while he looked up to check on the class and then quickly went back to his work.

Drew sat at her desk, staring at her empty journal page. She looked at the clock and saw she still had ten minutes left to write. She scanned the classroom. Her gaze landed on Nettie. Drew watched as Nettie wrote. She reached over and tapped Anna's shoulder. "What do you think she writes in there?" she whispered to Anna.

Nettie's ears perked at the sound of her name and as casually as possible she turned to see Drew and Anna whispering.

"Who knows?" Anna went back to writing.

"And who cares, right?" Drew rolled her eyes. Then she shrugged. "But I'm kind of curious. I mean what could *she* possibly have to write about?"

Nettie concealed a smile. She wanted to giggle. Drew was curious about her. *Interesting.*

"Maybe she writes about her brother. Or her father leaving. Wow, her life is really sad."

"Oh I know. Totally tragic," Drew agreed. "You'd think all that would make her, I don't know, interesting. But sadly, no. She's just a dork who's reading all the time." Another couples of minutes passed before Drew whispered to Anna again. "Can you see what she's writing?"

"No," Anna replied, not looking up from her paper.

Mr. Campbell, hearing the whispers, looked up to find Drew craning her neck towards Nettie. "Ms. Summers, is there something fascinating about Ms. Gaines?"

Drew sat up straight in her chair. "No, Mr. Campbell," she answered.

"You seem to be staring quite a bit." Nettie pretended to keep writing, not daring to glance over and see the look on Drew's face.

"It's nothing, sir," Drew answered in her best innocent voice.

"Well, next time, take a picture, it lasts longer. Now go back to writing." Mr. Campbell then said to the entire class, "Only seven minutes left."

It was impossible for Nettie not to smile. She took a quick glance at Drew. *Oops.* Drew was looking right at her. Nettie quickly looked back to her journal.

* * * *

January 14

The most hilarious thing is happening right now. It's journal time, obviously, because here I am writing. Anyway, I heard Drew and Anna whispering, trying to figure out what I was writing. And then Mr. Campbell caught them and totally humiliated them in front of the entire class. It was so great. I had to bite my lip to keep from laughing. I thought Drew might explode right there in her seat. I'm dying to look back and see if they're still staring at me. Finally, something embarrassing happens to someone other than me.

* * * *

"Okay, time is up. Put your journals away and pull out your math homework from last night." Mr. Campbell rose from his chair. "As usual, I'll be drawing names out of the hat and the lucky winners can come to the board and solve the problems for us. Remember, if you get stuck, you have one chance to ask for a hint and after that you're on your own. Each right answer is worth five extra credit points and don't forget to show all your work. If you did the homework, this should be a piece of cake."

Mr. Campbell reached into his hat and removed a piece of paper. "Our first lucky contestant is Ms. Gaines. You can do number seven. Next is Mr. Wyatt. You can do number fifteen, please."

Standing next to Andrew at the board, Nettie could not help but steal a few glances at him. When he caught her looking at him, she quickly turned her attention to the blackboard. Nettie picked up a piece of chalk, fumbled it in her hands, and dropped it on the floor. Without thinking, Andrew reached down, picked it up. As he handed it to her, his hand brushed against hers. Their eyes met. Nettie expected him to turn away quickly but he didn't. She smiled. To Nettie's surprise, Andrew smiled back.

Feeling her cheeks redden, Nettie turned away just in time to see Drew glaring at her.

Drew raised her hand. "Mr. Campbell, may I go to the bathroom?"

"Yes," Mr. Campbell answered.

Nettie completed the math problem, getting it right on the first try. She returned to her desk, basking in the glow of Andrew's smile and Drew's humiliation. She never noticed what was missing from her desk.

Chapter Fifteen
The Night Before

*U*nable to sleep, Nettie lay awake in her bed. She pushed aside the covers
*and tiptoed into the hall. Joe's bedroom light was on and so as she had
done many nights before, she crept into her brother's room.*

*Nettie poked her head in the door. "Joe? You awake?" Although the light
was still on, Joe had fallen asleep while doing his homework.*

*"I am now," he said, rubbing his eyes as he sat up. Even half asleep, Joe
was beautiful. His blond hair was mussed and flattened on one side. His
blue eyes, sleepy and half shut, looked like two aqua marbles. Even like this,
even looking like a total mess, his handsomeness took over. He had broad
shoulders and mountain ranges of muscles. To Nettie he was perfect and
she envied his perfection. He was everything she wasn't—beautiful, bold,
and athletic.*

*"Can I ask you something?" Nettie climbed up onto the edge of Joe's
bed.*

*"Sure, go ahead." He patted the bed. Nettie curled up next to him,
tucking her feet beneath his blankets.*

"Are you in love with Jenna?"

"Nettie it's late. Do we really have to talk about this now?"

"Please?"

"Okay. Yes, I'm in love with Jenna," Joe said with confidence.

"Do you tell her you love her?" Nettie asked.

*"Yes, I do." Nettie loved how honest he was with her. No matter what
she asked him, he always gave her an honest answer.*

"How do you know you're in love?" Nettie asked.

Joe shrugged as he said, "I don't know. I just know."

"But how do you know?"

Joe thought about his answer for a moment and then said, "Well, I like her. I like hanging out with her. I care about what happens to her."

"Do you kiss her?"

"Nettie!" Joe picked up his pillow and playfully swatted Nettie with it.

"Come on, tell me," Nettie pleaded.

"Yes, I kiss her. Now go to bed." Joe flopped down on his pillows.

"Okay, I will." Nettie got up to leave. She stopped and asked, "Joe? How will I know when I'm in love?"

"You'll just know. You'll get a feeling in your heart. And you'll think about the person all the time," Joe said.

"I think I love Andrew." It was the first time she'd ever said it to anyone.

"Nettie, you're only ten."

"I know. But I really do think I love him," Nettie defended herself.

"Okay. So you're in love. Go to sleep." Joe closed his eyes.

"Joe? Do you think Andrew loves me?"

"How should I know?"

"I don't know. How can I tell if he loves me?"

"If he loves you, he'll tell you, maybe not to your face, and he might not actually say it, but you'll be able to tell. Like when I wanted to show Jenna that I loved her, I did stuff for her, you know?"

"What kind of stuff?" Nettie asked.

"That's none of your business." Joe smiled broadly, remembering how he'd opened doors for her, carried stuff for her, and left little presents for her in her locker.

"Ah, come on Joe, tell me," Nettie begged.

"No. That's private," Joe stated firmly.

"Fine." Nettie gave up. "I guess I'll go to bed now. I love you Joe."

"Love you too."

* * * *

Do I like or object to change?

February 5

Everything in my life is changing, again. I know that things can't always stay the same, believe me, I learned that lesson the hard way. I just wish it didn't all happen so fast and all at the same time. My Mom and Chris are getting even closer and Elisa and Justin are practically glued together. Don't get me wrong, I'm happy for them. I just don't feel like I'm as big a part of their lives as I once was. I mean they include me as much as they can, but sometimes I feel like it's out of pity. It's great that the people around me are finding love. I'm happy that things are changing for them in that way. I just wish sometimes that their finding love didn't make me feel like I'm being left behind.

When I was younger I asked Joe about love. It was the last real conversation I had with him. I didn't realize that at the time. He died the next day. I remember talking to him like it was yesterday. He said it would happen for me someday. He said someday someone would love me. I guess I'm still waiting.

I don't like change very much. Not when change means loss. Mostly I want things to change back to the way they were before. I'm not sure if that counts.

Some people say change is about progress and that progress is good because it means expanding and building. But what happens to everything that gets destroyed in the wake of change? I wish there was some way to balance change and loss. That would certainly make my life easier.

CHAPTER SIXTEEN

WORD SPREADS FAST

After a trip to the bookstore, Nettie unloaded her purchases onto her bed. Nettie loved buying books. To her, there was nothing better than a new book. She read all the jacket covers before selecting which book to read first. Just as she settled in to begin a new journey, her doorbell rang. At first she thought about ignoring it, but it rang again. As Nettie went downstairs, the bell ringer began pounding on the front door.

"Nettie! Nettie! Open up!" Elisa yelled.

"I'm coming, I'm coming," Nettie answered back as she opened the door. "God, what is it? What's wrong?"

Elisa was out of breath and looked as if she had just run a marathon. "I got here as fast as I could. I ran all the way from my house. Can I come in?"

"Why didn't you just call me?" Nettie asked, stepping aside to let Elisa enter. They walked into the living room and sat down on the couch. "What's going on?"

"Something horrible has happened. Andrew broke up with Drew."

Nettie smiled. "I'm missing the horrible part."

"The horrible part is that Drew stole your journal." Elisa's chest heaved as she tried to catch her breath.

Nettie shook her head. "No she didn't. I've got it upstairs." Nettie rose from the couch and headed for her room. Elisa followed.

"Then she must've made a copy because she's got it and she's passing it out to our whole class!"

Nettie shook her head violently back and forth, trying to shake off the news. "That's impossible," she said as she retrieved the journal from her desk and hugged it to her chest.

"Justin called me a few minutes ago. He said he got out of basketball practice and there were copies sticking out of every locker."

"Why would she do that? How? I don't get it. What did I do to her?" The news sunk in and Nettie felt the crushing blow. Soon her entire class would know all the things she wrote about in her journal—her brother, her father. Andrew! She slumped onto her bed. "This can't be happening."

"Justin said he grabbed as many of them as he could but some of them were gone."

Nettie swallowed hard. She looked up at Elisa, her eyes full of tears. "Do you think Andrew read it?"

"I don't know. Maybe." Elisa sat down on the bed next to Nettie and put her arm around her. Nettie buried her face in her hands and cried. The journal slid to the floor. "I'm so sorry, Nettie."

Nettie practically jumped off the bed. Sadness turned to horror as she paced back and forth. She kept saying over and over, "I don't know what to do. I don't know what to do. How do I go to school tomorrow? How do I face everyone?"

"I don't know."

Chapter Seventeen
Facing The Day

Nettie did her best to convince her mom that she was sick. She tried everything to get out of going to school, but nothing worked. She even went so far as to go into the bathroom and fake vomiting noises. The irony is that if she had eaten anything in the last day she could've easily thrown up at this point. A part of her thought she should just tell her mom what had happened, that she'd been humiliated and her life was ruined. But she was afraid her mom would call Chris, and Nettie knew somehow that would be worse.

On the walk to school Nettie watched the other kids. She wondered what their lives were like. *Is anyone out there suffering like me? Doubtful.* She doubted that any kid had ever suffered as much as her. It wasn't enough for her brother to die, her father to leave, or to be made fun of because she liked to read. Now her innermost thoughts had been passed around for anyone to read and she couldn't understand why.

With a book positioned in front of her face, Nettie entered the school hall. If the kids were staring at her, she did her best not to notice. She headed for her locker. At first she didn't see what was taped to the front. As she got closer she could see that it was an entry from her journal. Without reading it, she tore it off. Nettie opened her locker and began her daily routine of unpacking her backpack and gathering her supplies for her first few classes. From behind her she could hear snickering. Bits and pieces of conversations buzzed her ears like flies. "So pathetic." "Seriously deluded." "Wow, sucks to be her." She wished she had a swatter for the unwanted noise.

Nettie heard Drew and Anna chatting away behind her. Without turning around, Nettie spoke to Drew. "Did you and Andrew really break up?" Nettie knew she shouldn't have asked but she couldn't help herself.

"Not for long. He'll come back to me." Drew looked Nettie up and down. "It's not like he'll ever go out with you anyway."

"I don't want to go out with him, Drew." Nettie's heart raced. She felt the tears building behind her eyes. She was tired of running, tired of hiding. Why did she allow this girl that she didn't even like torment her so? Why did she let her talk to her the way she did? *Enough!* She looked squarely at Drew. "Why'd you do it? Why'd you steal my journal?"

"I don't know what you're talking about," Drew lied, half smiling.

"Liar!" Nettie shouted as she stepped closer to Drew. Her book slammed to the floor. All the heads in the hall whipped around at the noise. "You already had Andrew. You didn't need to do this."

"Maybe he needed to know what you're really like." Drew was not backing down. "A sad loser whose mom is dating our teacher!" Kids surrounding them started to laugh.

Nettie's rage consumed her. "Fine, Drew. I'm a loser. Go ahead, laugh at me." She turned and looked at all those staring at her. "I hope it makes you feel great! I hope you all get a huge laugh out of it. If you're that threatened by me, go ahead." Nettie turned back and slammed her locker shut and tried to walk away.

Drew stood in her path. "Threatened? By you? Be serious! I'm not threatened by anyone." Drew stepped toward Nettie. They were practically nose to nose.

Her whole body tired, Nettie whispered, "Then why?"

Drew smiled. She tossed her hair over her shoulder, and stood with her hands on her hips. "Because I could." Drew's answer was more honest than Nettie expected.

At that moment Andrew walked into the hallway. Nettie waited for him to come to her defense. She wanted desperately for him to tell Drew off, for him to do anything that showed her he was still her friend.

"Hey Andrew! Did you see this?" Andrew's friend Charlie asked as he held up a copy of the journal.

Andrew looked at Nettie and said nothing. Nettie could tell by the look on his face that not only had he seen it, but he'd read it too. Nettie wanted to throw up and scream all at the same time. He walked toward her. He looked like he wanted to say something, but his friend Jake came over and he just walked away.

All this time Nettie knew that her friendship with Andrew had been changed. But she never wanted to believe it was over. She never wanted to look at Andrew and feel as disappointed as she did. Suddenly the bell rang, interrupting the scene. Nettie grabbed her stuff and hurried into the classroom.

Through out the day Nettie tried to concentrate, but to no avail. She couldn't help but wonder what had happened between Andrew and Drew. She desperately wanted to know what caused the breakup, but she knew there was no way to find out.

At one point during the day Drew was called out of the classroom to the principal's office. As she exited, Mr. Campbell put down his teacher's manual. He stood behind his podium and told everyone to close his or her books. He paused for what felt like ten minutes before he walked casually over to his desk and propped himself on it. He leaned back and folded his arms across his chest.

"Ladies and gentlemen, I think it's time we had a little chat," Mr. Campbell began. *Please don't mention my name. Please don't mention my name,* Nettie thought. "I want to explain something to you about how the world works. Right now, you're in eighth grade. You're on top of the world. You'll be graduating in a few months and heading off to high school. And eventually, you'll graduate from high school and go to college where you'll prepare for the rest of your lives. But really, that preparation starts here. It's important to learn now how to treat one another so that you can get through the rest of your lives. It might be easy now to pick on someone weaker then you, but that doesn't mean you should. Sometime in your life you might be the weaker person and you certainly wouldn't want someone taking advantage of you. We need to learn some common decency and respect for one another."

He paused, stood from his perched position and continued, "I am ashamed that a student from my class is responsible for not only stealing Nettie's journal, but then photocopying it for everyone to see. It's deplorable. It's evil and wrong and I'm extremely disappointed. You all owe Nettie an apology and I expect you to try to make amends. I will not tolerate this kind of behavior in my classroom and I'm telling you now that you do not want this kind of thing on your conscience. Eventually, it will come back to haunt you."

He paused again for a long time, looking at each student directly. He half smiled, eyes full of pity, at Nettie. She wished her chair would swallow her whole. Mr. Campbell returned to his podium and announced he was giving a pop quiz. The class groaned at first but then sensed rather quickly that Mr. Campbell was not in the mood to entertain their complaints. Each student removed a blank piece of paper from their desk and poised their pencils, waiting for the first question.

Although Drew missed Mr. Campbell's little speech, Nettie knew she'd hear about it from her friends. Nettie desperately wished that Mr. Campbell hadn't said anything at all. It would've been better that way. Nettie hated that everyone was talking about her. She especially hated listening to the whispers of how her "daddy," Mr. Campbell, stepped in to protect her.

Chapter Eighteen

The Funeral

Freewrite

March 30

People keep talking about high school and how they cannot wait for this year to be over. No one feels that way more than me. I can't wait to leave this place. I'm tired of being stuck here with all these people.

I hate my class. By now they've all read the journal and they know everything. All of my most private thoughts are on display for everyone to see. Now everyone knows how much I like Andrew. I just don't know what I did to deserve all of this. I hate being me. I'm cursed.

And I'm tired of feeling lonely! I can't tell my mom or Elisa about how truly lonely I am because then they'll just feel sorry for me. I really hate when people feel sorry for me. And right now everyone I know is either laughing at me behind my back or feeling sorry for me. Either way, it sucks.

I can't believe Drew did this to me. She humiliated me in front of Andrew. She humiliated me in front of everyone. But what really kills me is that Andrew knows the truth now. I get sick to my stomach thinking about how Andrew read all that stuff I wrote about him.

I don't know what to do now. What do I do? I wish my dad were here. I want my dad. I want Joe. I don't want to be here anymore. I don't want to be me anymore.

I want to go back to the way things were when
Andrew and I were friends. What happened to the boy
I used to know?

I feel like the world is spinning out of control and I
am powerless to stop it. I just want to run. The last time
I felt like this, it was Andrew who came to my rescue.
There's not much chance of that happening now.

* * * *

*The entire church was packed. Every seat was taken with people standing
two rows deep in the back. Nettie sat in the front row between
her mother and father. The sounds of whimpering and sniffling echoed
throughout the great hall. Nettie's eyes were dry and tired. Her black
velvet dress pulled at her neck. Her satin Mary Jane shoes squeezed her
toes together. In her mother's hands were wrinkled, partially used Kleenex.
Every so often her mother would sniff and bow her head to wipe her runny
nose. Nettie's father looked the most uncomfortable. He wrung his hands
and brushed his pant legs for nonexistent hairs. Whenever her father was
nervous he fidgeted, and her mother would always rest her hand on his
leg, calming him. Today, however, Nettie's parents sat together almost as
strangers, not paying attention to each other.*

*Nettie tried to find something in the church to focus on other than
the casket on the altar. She scanned the walls of the church, counting each
station of the cross and reciting the story in her head. She counted the
different colors in the stained glass windows. She watched as members of
the congregation filtered down the center aisle, leaving roses, footballs, and
other tokens of fond memories by the casket. Nettie felt overwhelmed by
the outpouring of love for her brother. She recognized some of his friends,
teammates mostly. There were teachers, parents, community members. It
seemed as if the entire town had turned out to say good-bye.*

*Steve Wyatt rose and walked to the dais. He thanked everyone for
coming and for all their love and support. He expressed the gratitude of the
Gaines family and invited everyone to the luncheon after the services. When
the pleasantries were finished, Steve Wyatt pulled from his breast pocket a
neatly folded piece of paper. He paused for a moment to wipe his eyes and
clear his throat before beginning the eulogy.*

*"I've known Dan and Annie Gaines since they were college sweethearts.
They are the perfect parents. And they don't deserve to be here now, mourning
the loss of their boy, Joe. As Joe's godfather, I loved him like he was my own.*

I watched him grow into a fine young man and a tremendous athlete. No one loved life more than Joe. His passion and his heart were inspiring. He will be deeply missed by me and by all of us. I think the appropriate way to honor Joe is not with tears and sad good-byes. Joe wouldn't like the idea of causing so much sadness. He'd want to know that we cherish his memory and he'd want each of us to take a piece of him with us, whether it be his generosity, his spirit, his zest for life, or his love for his family and friends. Nettie, Andrew, Jenna, I'm sure this tragedy is frightening. To lose someone you love at such a young age is never easy for anyone, let alone children. Joe loved you three, his kid sister, his buddy, and his first love. It will be difficult for you three to adjust to such a loss, but just know that he loved you and he would've wanted you guys to stick together, now more than ever. And to Annie and Dan, whose hearts must be breaking, you raised an amazing man whom we are all so proud of. Thank you for sharing him with us, for allowing us to be in his great presence, even if it was for a short sixteen years."

A few of Joe's friends and football buddies spoke as well. Nettie listened to them talk about how much they loved and respected Joe; how they would all miss him. A few of his classmates read poems and his teachers talked about how he was such a dedicated student. At the end of the service, the priest nodded to Nettie letting her know it was time. Nettie stepped forward and took her place at the microphone.

As the organist played the opening bars, Nettie thought back to a conversation she'd had with Joe many years before. They had been sitting in his room listening to the radio when one of their great-grandmother's songs came on. Nettie sang along without really thinking about it until she noticed Joe staring at her.

"What?" she asked self-consciously, "Why are you looking at me?"

Joe looked amazed. "I didn't know you could sing like that."

"Like what?" Nettie asked nervously.

"Like G.G. You sound just like her."

"I do not." She rolled her eyes and playfully slapped Joe's shoulder.

Joe looked at Nettie very seriously and said, "Nettie, you sound just like her. It's actually a little creepy how much you sound like her. You have a beautiful voice. Promise me kid, you'll sing at my wedding and my funeral." Nettie nodded in agreement, thinking her big brother was too kind.

Nettie stood at the microphone and remembered that promise to Joe. She wanted nothing more than to sing for Joe, to say good-bye in her own special way, in the way he asked of her. Both her parents had tried to stop her. They told her it was too much for her and that if she didn't want to sing, Joe would understand.

Despite their efforts to dissuade her, Nettie assured them that this was something she wanted to do. And in her heart she knew it was something she had to do, for Joe. But as she stood there with everyone looking at her she was overcome with grief. Her heart pounded in her chest. Her hands dampened with sweat. Her knees buckled from under her and she fell to the ground sobbing. The next thing she knew she was being lifted from the altar.

When she woke, she was at home, lying on her bed. She must have passed out. Still in her black dress and shoes, she went to her bedroom door and opened it just a crack. The noise of guests filled the house with the quiet hum of whispers. Feeling unable to join them, she closed the door and leaned her forehead against it. Again she felt hot, and her heart pounded. She couldn't face them. She went to her closet, opened the door, and climbed inside.

The door to the closet opened and Nettie looked up to see Andrew looking back at her. He said nothing, just moved some clothes aside and sat down next to her. They sat in silence and sadness. Nettie hadn't noticed when Andrew took her hand. She just looked down and saw her hand in his, like it had been there the whole time.

PART TWO
ANDREW

CHAPTER NINETEEN

WHO AM I?

At the start of the new school year, Andrew Wyatt vowed to make a change. This year, things would be different. He was gently encouraged to make a change by his father. Well, threatened was more like it. His father had told him in no uncertain terms that he was not going to put up with any more mischief from Andrew and his two "yokel" friends, as his father called them. Andrew was warned that one call from the principal's office meant no football camp in the summer.

Andrew stood with his two yokel friends, Charlie Mitchell and Jake Allen, waiting for the bell signaling the beginning of the eighth grade year. Students huddled together in their usual crowds, nerds with nerds, jocks with jocks. He noticed right away when Nettie arrived. She walked across the blacktop, a book between her hands, paying no attention to the world around her, not even the football slung between two seventh graders that narrowly missed colliding with her face.

Drawn back into conversation he heard Charlie say, "There goes Nosey."

"It's too bad she's such a geek, she's kind of pretty in a pre-makeover kind of way," Jake added.

"Pre-makeover? Someone's been watching 'Queer Eye for the Straight Guy' again." Charlie nudged his friend.

"Hey, I told you my cousin was on it. Besides, there's nothing wrong with a dude knowing how to dress. That's how I get all the ladies." Jake puffed out his chest proudly.

"Yeah right." Charlie laughed and Jake socked him in the arm. "Andrew here is the only one with a chick. So give it up." Charlie said to Andrew, "how's the action with Drew?"

Andrew breathed a sigh of relief as the bell rang, ending their conversation and rescuing him from having to answer.

Mr. Campbell, the new teacher, gave instructions to pick a seat, which Andrew did mindlessly and only half listening. He was too busy watching Nettie. She looked completely at home in a classroom. Andrew secretly envied her enthusiasm for schoolwork, something he lacked entirely. Schoolwork had never been his thing. It was Nettie's thing. He used to enjoy watching her speed through spelling tests. He thought it was hilarious when she corrected a teacher.

After a notebook appeared in front of him, Andrew snapped back from his thoughts and realized that he had an assignment to complete. Since it was the first day of school, Andrew had hoped to skate by without much heavy thinking and definitely without homework. He had the sinking feeling that he wasn't going to be quite so lucky.

He exhaled deeply and frowned a bit at Mr. Campbell's instruction to write an essay entitled, "Who am I?" Andrew thought about the question for a moment, not having a clue where to begin. He'd never given a single thought before now about who he was. In fact, he'd avoided thinking about himself in any sort of context other than football player, for fear of what the real answer might be.

Who am I?

August 30

I am Andrew Michael Wyatt. I am thirteen years old and an eighth grader at St. Elizabeth's. I like to play football. I think I'm pretty good at it. I'm not as good as I'd like to be, but I'm working on it.

Every year I go to football camp and this summer I made starting quarterback. I remember the day they announced the teams, I could hardly believe it when they called my name. They gave me Joe's old number, which at first didn't feel right, but it would've felt really weird if they'd given it to someone else.

I learned almost everything I know about football from my friend Joe. I wish he were still around to teach me more. Joe died about three years ago in a car accident. I never really thought about it before, but Joe was a big part of who I was before he died. He was my hero, I guess. I kind of worshipped him like he was a rock star or something. (My sister Jenna used to say that to me all the time, but I never really thought it was true before now.)

I used to be friends with Joe's sister, Nettie. But after Joe died, I just kind of stopped. I don't really know why. We don't really have any of the same friends at school and once our families stopped spending so much time together, we stopped being friends. She probably doesn't even wonder why we're not friends anymore. I know she thinks I'm a jerk now.

I don't mean to be a jerk. I just kind of go along with my friends, and if we end up getting in trouble, so what? It's not like I'm perfect, like Joe. I tried to be like Joe for a long time, but I'm not Joe and I'm never going to be, so why bother trying? It doesn't matter anyway. I don't really care what she thinks about me.

Chapter Twenty

Planet of the Eighth Graders

The cafeteria was one of Andrew's least favorite places on campus. He hated the noise, the chaos, the greasy food. He wished he could just sit outside in the quad under a tree by himself. He felt irritated having to sit with his friends Jake and Charlie, watching them fire spit wads around the room or snort milk through their noses. Lunchtime was the only time Andrew saw Jake and Charlie for who they were, six-year-olds trapped in thirteen-year-old bodies, and he didn't like it. He didn't want to think about how immature they acted because then he had to think about how immature he acted when he was around them.

Another thing Andrew didn't like about lunchtime was having his girlfriend, Drew, hang all over him like a heavy, wet blanket. He somehow always felt like a fire hydrant and she was a dog, peeing all over him and marking her territory. Sometimes he just wanted to scream, "Enough already!" The entire school knew they were going out and he hated the way she rubbed it in their faces like he was some carnival prize she'd won. Andrew recalled his horror when he read Drew's MySpace page the day he asked her out. She wallpapered her front page with Photoshopped pictures of the two of them standing together on the beach, in front of the Eiffel Tower, and at Disneyland.

Drew smothered him, playing with his hair, jabbing him in the stomach. He wouldn't admit it to anyone, but Drew's playful little slaps left welts across his torso. Andrew especially didn't like the way Drew tortured Nettie with their relationship. Andrew knew Nettie could care less who he dated so he never really understood why Drew was always trying to throw it in her face.

"Look, Andrew." Drew ran her hand along Andrew's biceps. "She's staring at us again."

Andrew looked over at Nettie just in time to see her knock over her milk carton and spill milk all over the table.

"Give it a rest, Drew."

"God, you're so touchy when it comes to her. You know she's like totally obsessed with you."

"Whatever," Andrew muttered as he shoved a handful of chips in his mouth.

"I'm serious. She's always looking at us. You know she's jealous because she totally wants to be your girlfriend. But you're already taken, aren't you?"

"Uh-huh." Andrew looked down at where his watch should be, remembering only then that Drew had insisted on wearing it today. He silently urged the bell to ring.

"She's pathetic. I mean yeah, you guys used to be friends, but that's only because your parents forced you to be friends with her. She should just get over it. Don't you think?" Andrew said nothing. He watched as Nettie and Elisa prepared to exit the room.

"Andrew, are you listening to me? I'm trying to talk to you. It's so uncool of her to drool over my boyfriend. I'm not going to let her get away with it," Drew hissed.

"Leave her alone, Drew. She's harmless. And she could probably care less about us."

"You could not be more wrong. I'm telling you that she wants you. Everyone knows this but you."

The bell rang, again rescuing Andrew from a conversation he did not want to be having. He packed up his things and headed out of the cafeteria. He made it back to the classroom before the second bell rang, but not before he overheard Drew sniping at Nettie in the hall.

Chapter Twenty-One

It Happened One Night

Andrew woke to the sound of the front door slamming shut. He rolled over and checked the clock. 1:23 AM. He grabbed a T-shirt from the hamper and trudged downstairs to find his father and his sister standing in the kitchen.

"So where's the party?" Andrew asked sarcastically as he grabbed himself a glass from the cupboard and made his way to the sink to get some water.

"Do you know anything about our house being TP'd?" Steve Wyatt asked.

"I've been sleeping."

"Jenna, what do you know about this?"

"Nothing, Dad, I swear."

"Well, the two of you are going to clean this mess up tomorrow."

"Dad, that is completely unfair! Why should I be punished for something I didn't even do?" Jenna crossed her arms across her chest.

"Do either of you recognize this backpack?" Steve held up the plain black backpack for them to inspect. At the sight of it, Andrew almost spit out his water.

There were no significant markings on the bag, and Andrew couldn't be sure it belonged to who he thought until he got a better look at it.

"I don't know, Dad. But I do know it wasn't any of my friends. In our class the guys TP the girl's house to ask them to the Grad Dance. So I seriously doubt it was anyone I know," Andrew said.

"It wouldn't be your little girlfriend?' Jenna asked with just a hint of accusation.

"I don't think so. It was probably one of your friends."

"My friends are too mature to do something like this!"

"Are you talking about the same mature friends who filled the fountain at the country club with goldfish last year?" Andrew knew that would get her.

"Enough, you two. We're not going to settle this tonight. Let's get some sleep and we'll figure this out in the morning," Steve instructed.

"I'll be right up. I need a snack."

"Andrew, it's late." His father motioned to his watch.

"I know, but I got home late from practice and I'm still starving."

"You're just like I was at your age. The stomach that never sleeps. There's some leftover pizza in the fridge. But don't be too long." With that, Steve and Jenna retreated to their rooms.

Andrew wasn't hungry. He waited until he heard the bedroom doors closing before he went over to the backpack, now lying on the kitchen table, and picked it up. Slowly, he unzipped the small exterior pocket. He folded back the material as best he could and saw exactly what he'd been looking for. In small gold etching was the number 12, Joe's football number. He was right. It was Nettie's backpack. And he knew exactly where to look for her.

The Dennison's house was just a few short blocks from his own, and in his pajamas and bare feet, Andrew managed to make it there just in time to catch Nettie and Elisa making their escape.

He hadn't known what he was going to say to her if and when he caught her. He didn't know why he was even angry. But when he saw her he felt consumed with anger, and before he knew it bile was spewing from his mouth. He said awful things, hurtful things to her, and before he could take it back, she unloaded on him with her full arsenal.

The first bullet—that she hated him—struck him in the stomach, and if he could he would've stumbled backward. The next shot she fired—that he thought he was too good for her—hit him in the shoulders, making him stiffen. A bad taste bubbled up from his stomach to his mouth. But the last shot—the bullet that struck him in the heart, with the intent to slaughter—was when she mentioned Joe.

He left, wounded, and without saying anything more.

* * * *

Freewrite

October 10
I spent the weekend clearing my front yard of toilet paper. It sucked. My house was TP'd by Nettie. I haven't

told anyone that I know it was her. Drew's been going crazy trying to figure it out, so finally I told her that it was one of my sister's friends. I'd hate to see what she'd do to Nettie if she found out the truth.

I've been really trying not to think about it, but Nettie said something to me that night that stuck in my head like a bad song or something. She said something about wishing Joe could see what kind of person I turned out to be. It's got me thinking, if Joe were here, what would he think of me? He'd hate me. I know it.

He'd hate me for the way I treat his sister, for not looking out for her like I always said I would. I let him down. I'm nothing like Joe. I'm not the stand-up guy or the generous guy. I'm not responsible or trustworthy. I'm not a good friend. I'm not even a good boyfriend.

I'm really glad Joe isn't here to see me now. But he's watching me. Right? That's what people always say when someone dies, that they are still watching us. If that's true, I doubt he likes what he sees.

CHAPTER TWENTY-TWO

HAPPY NEW YEAR

Andrew dressed for the evening in a pair of dark, slightly baggy jeans and a long-sleeved blue dress shirt, which he left untucked. He brushed his teeth and thought back to the phone conversation he'd had about New Year's Eve with Drew.

"You're going to a party without me?" Drew pouted.

"It's not really a party. And it's at Nettie's. Why would you want to go?"

"It's New Year's Eve, Andrew. We're supposed to be together."

"Look Drew, it's no big deal."

"It is a big deal. And I'm hurt that you don't understand that. I think it will be fun to go to Nettie's."

"You want to go to Nettie's?" Andrew asked suspiciously.

"Of course. If it means I get a New Year's Eve kiss from you. Besides, I think Nettie and I could really be friends if we tried."

"Drew, I'm not sure Nettie would feel very comfortable with you there."

"Well, it's not really about her. Is it Andrew? It's about me. I'm your girlfriend, and I don't think it's very considerate of you to go to another girl's party without me."

"Fine, Drew. You can come. But you'll try to be nice, right?"

"Andrew. Please. I'm always nice."

Drew's parting words hung over Andrew like a dark rain cloud waiting to burst. She was never nice to Nettie and Andrew knew it. But he thought as long as he was at the party with Drew she might behave herself.

They arrived at Nettie's around 7:45. The house was full of guests. Nettie greeted them at the door looking nothing like she normally did.

Her blonde hair, usually worn in a ponytail, hung in ringlets around her shoulders. She wasn't wearing makeup, but the warmth from the party gave her cheeks a rosy glow. She looked genuinely happy, with a sweet, inviting smile. Her hazel eyes squeezed shut as his parents each hugged her. Andrew could tell that she felt right at home with his parents, like family.

Drew had never been too intent on impressing Andrew's family. His mother never expressed her disapproval vocally, but Andrew knew she didn't like her. He also knew without a doubt that his parents loved Nettie.

Andrew flinched as Drew thrust her coat at Nettie. He knew right then that it had been a mistake to bring her. He thought maybe he would find Nettie later and tell her that he hadn't wanted to bring her and that she'd basically forced him to invite her. He wanted to explain to her that he hadn't wanted to hurt her, not tonight, not ever. When Andrew thought of all the things he wanted to or should say to Nettie his head swirled.

"*Oh my God*!" Drew yelled in Andrew's direction. "Can you believe this? Nettie's mom is dating Mr. Campbell. Oh, this is just too funny."

"Why is it funny?" Andrew was a little shocked by the sight of Nettie's mom dancing with their teacher, but mostly he wondered how Nettie must feel about this.

He'd never talked to her about her father leaving, but he knew it must've hurt very badly. He remembered, like it was yesterday, overhearing his parents talking about it.

* * * *

"Annie just called." Steve Wyatt placed the phone back on the cradle.
"And?" Sharon asked.
"Dan left."
"What?"
"Shh! I don't want the kids to hear."
Andrew, who'd been on his way to the kitchen with his dirty dishes, stopped, frozen against the wall, and listened.
"Oh my God, Steve. This is terrible. What else did she say?"

"She said that she came home from work and all his things were gone. He left a note on the table saying he was sorry, but that he just couldn't do it anymore." Steve shook his head in disbelief.

"Have you heard from him?"

"No. I hope he calls, though, so I can talk some sense into him. What the hell can he be thinking?"

"Oh, Steve. I know this is hard for you. Dan is your friend. But let's face it. He and Annie haven't been getting along for a while now."

"They've gone through hell, Sharon. After Joe died, I can't even imagine what that must've felt like. But they should've stuck together."

"I love what a romantic you are, Steven Wyatt. You are the most wonderful and sensitive man I've ever met. But honey, be honest, Dan and Annie weren't getting along before Joe died either."

Andrew's mouth hung open in shock. He hadn't known that. But why would he? Nettie hadn't mentioned anything about her parents not getting along. Why hadn't she said anything?

Andrew thought about how much had changed since Joe died. Before, he and Nettie had been so close. They told each other everything. He could tell her things he wouldn't dare tell his guy friends. He never told her how much he liked having her for a friend. He hadn't spent much time with her since Joe died. He knew he should call her, and tell her how bad he felt that her dad was leaving. But what would he say?

* * * *

My Christmas Vacation

January 1

The New Year's Eve party at Nettie's didn't go as smoothly as I hoped. I am such an idiot for bringing Drew. What was I thinking? I wasn't thinking. For a while now my dad's been kind of ragging on me and telling me that I don't think before I act. I just thought he was on my case; I didn't think he might actually be right. I hate it when parents are right about stuff.

Being in Nettie's house again made me think about a lot of things. Mostly it made me think about Drew. I don't know why I'm going out with her. I don't know if I ever really liked her. I thought we'd have stuff in common because she plays volleyball and I play football, but we don't.

I don't like who I am with her. I haven't liked myself in a very long time. I just didn't want to admit it I guess. I told my dad that this year I really would make some changes. My first change is going to be breaking up with Drew. This is gonna suck.

Chapter Twenty-Three

It's Over

After school, Andrew shot hoops in his backyard. He hadn't noticed Drew come through the gate until she spoke. "Hiya."

"Hey." Andrew tried not to appear uncomfortable. He hadn't wanted Drew to come over, but now that she was here, this was his opportunity to end things with her.

He was about to start when Drew asked, "Andrew, what do you think of Nettie?"

"I don't know." Andrew brushed off the question and retied his shoelace.

Drew flirtingly nudged his shoulder. "Come on. I'm just curious."

Andrew shrugged. "I don't really think about her." He tried not to look at Drew for fear she'd know he was lying.

"Why not? You've known her forever. You guys were friends for a really long time." Drew waited a few seconds before adding, "Plus, you know she's in love with you."

Andrew stopped dribbling and the ball rolled away. "What?"

"Oh please, you know she is. She wrote about it in her journal."

It took Andrew a moment to realize the weight of what Drew had said before asking, "How do you know? Did you read her journal?" Andrew knew Drew didn't like Nettie, but he thought this was a low blow even for her.

"Um, sort of. I actually photocopied it as a joke." Drew forced a laugh, "Wanna see?" she asked as she unzipped her backpack and removed the photocopied pages.

"No," Andrew said sternly as he retrieved his basketball.

Drew dangled the journal in front of Andrew. "You're not at all interested in what she said about you?"

"Did you show that to anyone?" Andrew feared the answer.

"Of course!" Drew laughed. "It's hilarious. You should really read it."

"How did you even get it?" Andrew yelled.

"I took it. Look, don't get all pissy at me. I did you a favor. This girl is practically drooling over you. And if she didn't want anyone to see it, why would she write it in her school journal?"

"Um, maybe because she thought it was private. No one is supposed to read that," Andrew snapped, "least of all you."

"What's that supposed to mean?" Drew looked hurt.

"That was really low, Drew."

Andrew started to walk away and Drew quickly moved to block his path. "Why do you care so much? Do you like her or something?" Drew was getting angry now.

"No. I don't," Andrew said firmly.

"Then why do you care so much?"

"Because I'm a decent human being." These words stung Drew and Andrew knew it. He took a moment before saying, "Drew, she and I were friends, a long time ago. We're not really anything anymore. You know that." Andrew shook his head as he said, "You shouldn't have taken her journal." Again, Andrew tried to leave.

Drew grabbed his arm and spun him around. "You're so naïve Andrew. Grow up! This girl is totally infatuated with you and you know it. You probably even like it. And I don't know why. She's such a disaster. Her own father doesn't even like her enough to hang around."

Andrew's eyes widened, his nostrils flared. "What'd you just say?"

"It's all here in the journal, Andrew. How after her brother died her father took off. Apparently he didn't want to be the father of such a loser."

"Shut up, Drew! Just shut up," Andrew fumed.

"Don't tell me to shut up. No one tells me to shut up. Besides, I'm just quoting from the journal. See what a loser she is?" Drew opened the journal to show Andrew a page.

"Don't call her a loser," Andrew said in low voice.

"Or what? I swear Andrew! You don't see what this girl does to you. I'm glad you're not friends with her anymore. You're too good for her anyway." Drew softened her tone and placed her arms around Andrew's neck. "Hey, I didn't mean for you to get all mad and defensive. I just wanted you to know that she wants to break us up. Don't let that happen, okay?" She kissed him lightly on the lips. He pushed her off.

"You really should read the journal. You have a right to know what she's saying about you. She TP'd your house, you know, trying to make it look like I did it. So don't think I'm the only nasty one here."

Andrew reluctantly took the journal from Drew before saying, "I don't want to be your boyfriend anymore."

"Excuse me?" Drew said furiously.

"I don't think we should be together anymore."

"Why? Because of Nettie?"

"No."

Drew's cheeks grew red. "Fine. Be with Nerdy. You two losers deserve each other," she said as she stormed out of the yard.

CHAPTER TWENTY-FOUR
TEMPTATION

Andrew Wyatt sat alone in his bedroom. Across the room on his desk lay the copy of Nettie's journal. He knew he shouldn't have it. He only had the journal because Drew stole it. The idea that Drew could be so cruel disgusted him. Andrew knew Drew could be a bit harsh, but he never thought she'd do something so deliberate, so mean. He rolled over on his bed, facing away from the journal. But he couldn't get it out of his mind. He had to do something. He crossed the room, picked up the journal, and threw it in the trash. Then he went over to the stereo and turned it on. The sounds of The Killers filled the room as Andrew tried to force the temptation out of his head. He knew he shouldn't read it. He knew it was wrong. The journal was full of Nettie's private thoughts and he had no right to violate them.

Suddenly, he felt a deep sadness, an empty feeling in the pit of his stomach. He hadn't allowed himself to think of Nettie or Joe in a very long time. He kept their memories locked away together in a tiny box inside his brain. It hurt too much to think about that box, tucked away and growing cobwebs. His heart told him to open the box, but his mind was screaming no. Could he go there? Could he think about Joe again? Could he think about Nettie? He pictured Nettie in his mind. She was ten with cute glasses and a fun smile. She was pretty. Her hazel eyes were his favorite part. He loved the flecks of gold in them; it made him think of buried treasure. A smile stretched across his mouth. He kept the picture in his mind and was surprised by all the memories that came flooding in.

He missed her. He hadn't let himself think that before, but now he couldn't help it. He missed the way they used to laugh and hang out and just be normal together. With her, he could just be himself. He wondered, *Did she miss him too? Or did she hate him?* He had to know. He stared at the garbage can. He couldn't help feeling curious. Had Nettie really written about him or was Drew lying? It would be like Drew to lie. She was probably lying. But how would he know unless he read it? He couldn't stand it any longer. He went to the garbage can and retrieved the journal. Opening it slowly, Andrew recognized the familiar handwriting. He sat back down on his bed and began to read an entry from November.

* * * *

November 17

I've tried really hard to forget about Andrew. After the way he treated me I should never talk to him again. I still can't believe I told him that I hate him because I don't. I'm trying to, but I can't. I've imagined myself as Andrew's girlfriend since I was six years old. He's part of me. I don't have any memories before the age of ten that don't include him. How am I supposed to just forget?

The first time I knew I loved him was when we were climbing the huge tree in my backyard and I slipped and fell. Everyone said I was lucky because I wasn't very high up so the fall wasn't that far. But I broke my ankle. I remember trying really hard not to cry, but it hurt so badly. Andrew came and sat by me. He told me everything was going to be okay. He came with me to the hospital and he sat with me while they put my cast on. He was the first one to sign it for me. He used to be so nice to me.

I know that we don't exactly travel in the same social circles anymore, but I don't understand what happened. We used to be so close and now ... now we're nothing to each other?

* * * *

Andrew felt his stomach tighten. Reading this journal was going to be harder than he thought.

He closed his eyes and remembered the day Nettie fell out of the tree. Andrew and Nettie had been sitting in her backyard watching Joe play football with some of his friends. Andrew climbed the tree first, trying to show off in front of Joe. Nettie followed. The tree branches hung low from the weight of the spring leaves. It was easy enough to get started climbing with the huge knothole that made the perfect perch. From there it was a bit trickier. Once Andrew made it to the top he reached back to help Nettie climb. At first he had a good grip on her. But his hands were sweaty and he couldn't hold on. He let go as her foot slipped. She screamed as she fell.

Joe came running. He cradled Nettie in his arms and carried her into the house. Andrew remembered how brave she'd been and how he too had tried to be brave while all the time he wanted to cry. He was so scared. He looked at Joe—so strong, so eager to help and to do the right thing.

Joe was Andrew's hero. *And Nettie is just like him*, Andrew thought, *helpful, considerate, a good person*. Even then Andrew knew Nettie was a better person than him, smarter, more honest. He tried to keep up with her and Joe. He wanted so much to be like them, to be good like them. He couldn't remember why or when he gave up trying.

Andrew flipped the journal to an October entry.

* * * *

Family Memories

October 25

Mr. Campbell gave us a prompt today. We're supposed to write about a happy memory with our family. I am having a hard time finding one. I can remember a time that was supposed to be happy. Joe's sixteenth birthday. My dad wanted to get him a Mustang and my mom didn't. Eventually he talked her into it. God, Joe loved that car. He took Jenna, Andrew, and me for a ride in it. It really went fast, but Joe was responsible and a good driver. No one knew he was going to die a week later in a car accident.

* * * *

Andrew remembered the car well. He could still smell the leather seats. He thought about how Joe washed it every day the first and only week he had it. Andrew shuddered, imagining what that gorgeous car must've looked like wrapped around a tree. He didn't want to think about it. He turned the pages to January

* * * *

Freewrite

January 12

Things have settled down a little since New Year's. It's weird to say, but I'm getting used to having Chris around the house. It almost feels like family.

I'm sad that Elisa and I aren't spending much time together. Things are different between us. She's been spending a lot of time with Justin and I don't like to tag along with them.

I don't see her very much after school anymore because I've been concentrating on my music lessons with Mrs. Morgan. Chris arranged for Mrs. Morgan to give me voice lessons twice a week. I love singing! I hadn't realized how much until now. Mrs. Morgan is a really great teacher. She makes me feel totally comfortable. I can't really explain it but somehow it makes me feel better knowing I can just go into the music room and let it all out. No matter what's happened during the day, when I'm singing there's nothing else in the world but the music and me.

* * * *

Overcome with guilt, Andrew closed the book. Memories flooded his mind and overwhelmed him. He lay on his bed forcing himself not to cry. He rose from the bed and walked toward his dresser. He opened the bottom drawer. He removed a pile of unfolded T-shirts and set them on the floor. He took out the drawer, flipped it over, and removed the picture he'd taped to the bottom. It was taken at the New Year's Eve party before Joe died. There they were, Joe and Jenna, the happy couple, beside them Andrew and Nettie smiling as wide as they could. What Andrew loved about the picture was that he was not looking at the camera. He was looking at Joe. He thought about how he too had really lost a brother. Andrew wondered what Joe would think of him now. How could he have let him down so badly?

Andrew thought back to the day of Joe's funeral. He remembered how packed the church was and how small he felt in such a large room. It was hard at the time to understand what really happened. How could one person be perfectly healthy and alive one day and not the next? It didn't seem right. He remembered sitting behind Nettie, uncomfortable in a suit that was too small and a tie that was practically choking him, wishing they could be sitting together underneath the apple tree instead of sitting in a cramped church. His mother told him several times that he didn't have to wear the suit, but in his mind he had to.

He wanted to wear it for Joe. Andrew knew that Nettie made a promise to sing for Joe. So he thought if she could get up in front of all those people, the least he could do was be uncomfortable in his clothes.

Andrew remembered how he'd stared to cry. He sniffled and sobbed quietly, hoping with all his heart that Nettie didn't turn around and see him. She didn't. She didn't even notice when he rushed to the altar after she collapsed. He'd been so scared for her. He wanted to help her in some way, but all he could do was watch as her father scooped her up and carried her out of the church.

After the funeral they'd all gone to Nettie's house. He remembered how when he got there Nettie was nowhere in sight. Annie had been looking for her for ten minutes when Andrew arrived.

Andrew knew exactly where she'd be. He took the stairs two at a time until he reached the landing. Without knocking, he entered Nettie's room. He took a deep breath before he tapped on her closet door. She didn't answer but he could hear her inside. Andrew reached for Nettie's hand and he held it for what felt like forever. Eventually, Andrew's father found them and made them come downstairs for food.

It was the last time he'd been a friend to her. Thinking all these thoughts, Andrew could no longer hold back the tears. For the second time, he cried over the loss of Joe. But this time, he cried for something else as well. For the first time, Andrew cried over the loss of Nettie.

The phone rang, interrupting his thoughts.

CHAPTER TWENTY-FIVE

MISSING

"Hello?" Andrew answered.

"Andrew? It's Annie. Is Nettie there by any chance?"

"No. Why?" Andrew sounded confused. Nettie hadn't been to the Wyatt house in over a year. Andrew wondered why Annie would think she'd be there.

"I can't find her."

"Did you call Elisa?"

"Just a minute ago. She hasn't heard from her either."

Andrew could hear the worry in Annie's voice as she asked, "Is your dad there?"

"Yeah, hang on." Andrew's stomach churned. A wave of panic washed over him. He raced up the stairs to his father's study. Without knocking he threw open the door. Mr. Wyatt practically jumped out of his skin. "Andrew?"

"Dad something's wrong. Annie's on the phone."

"What is it?" he asked with concern.

"I don't know. Hurry." They ran from the study together. By the time Steve Wyatt said hello, Annie was sobbing.

"Annie, Annie. Calm down. I can't understand what you're saying." He listened intently for a few moments and said, "Don't worry. I'll be right there. We'll find her. I promise we'll find her. She's probably just at a friend's house. I'm coming right now."

"Dad?"

"Annie can't find Nettie. But I'm sure everything is all right." Steve Wyatt retrieved his coat from the hall closet. He grabbed his car keys off the table and headed for the door.

"I'm coming with you." Andrew followed.

Steve paused. He placed his hands on Andrew's shoulders. "Just stay here in case she calls. Please. I'll call you as soon as she is home."

"Dad, I want to help." Andrew's voice broke. His father leaned forward and hugged him. "She's fine, Andrew. She's fine."

After his dad left, Andrew paced the living room floor. The thought of something happening to Nettie was more then he could bear. In that moment something became very clear to him. She was more than a friend and he knew it. He had been trying to deny it, but it was no use anymore. He knew he could not lose her now, not without telling her how he felt. He had to find her. Suddenly, he had an idea. He grabbed his coat and ran out the front door.

As he ran down the street it started to rain. He didn't care. He just kept running. His hair was drenched and stuck to his forehead. He blinked back tears and raindrops. He kept running. He ran with purpose and determination. Sycamore Street and left on Fifth. Past Trinity Church and the Nineteenth Street Theater. He followed as the road made a slight right curve and he stopped. Just for a moment. To catch his breath. At the T intersection of Fifth and Main. He was almost there.

He stopped running when he reached the gates. The rain beat down on him in a constant stream. Andrew walked slowly. He didn't want to scare her. He knew she'd be there. He'd seen her there before, talking to Joe. Every year, on Joe's birthday, Andrew went to the cemetery. He stayed back, not wanting to disturb Nettie and her mom. He thought Nettie saw him this year, standing behind a tree. She'd looked right at him. But she turned and walked away without saying anything.

He headed up the hill. When he didn't see her right away, his heart jumped. But as he got closer he saw the small figure of a girl huddled by the headstone.

Not knowing quite what to say, Andrew didn't say anything. He sat down beside her on the soggy ground. Nettie lifted her head only slightly.

She was crying. Her blond hair was soaked. She was shivering. Andrew wondered how long she had been here. He sat beside her, inching closer until their shoulders touched. Even though they were both cold and wet, when they touched they felt warm.

Without a word, Andrew slid his hand into Nettie's until his fingers were entangled with hers. He gave a little squeeze. She gave a little squeeze back. They sat there, huddled together for what felt like an eternity. Andrew knew he should call Annie or his dad, and tell them where they were, but he also knew Nettie wasn't ready to go home.

Finally, he spoke. "Nettie, are you okay?" Immediately he knew it was a stupid question. Obviously she was not okay. "Your mom is looking for you." Nettie said nothing, "Come on, I'll take you home."

Together they walked back, still holding hands. As they stood at her front door Andrew began to say something as the door flew open.

"Oh my God!" Annie yelled. She grabbed her daughter and hugged her with all her might. "Thank God. Nettie, where were you? Are you okay?" Nettie's mother ushered her into the house. Nettie looked back at Andrew, still standing on the front porch. Annie didn't seem to notice him and she closed the door behind them.

CHAPTER TWENTY-SIX
OLD FRIENDS

Early the next morning, Andrew made the short walk from his house to Nettie's. Annie greeted him at the front door with a hug and a warm smile. She told him that Nettie was in her room and that he could go on up and see her.

"Nettie, can I come in?" Andrew asked as he tapped on the door.

"Yeah, it's open."

He wiped his sweaty palms on his jeans before turning the knob. "Hey," he said as he walked into the room. "You okay?"

"Yeah, um, I'm okay I guess." Nettie nodded. Andrew knew she was shocked to see him and doing her best to remain calm.

"I, uh, I'm sorry about the whole journal thing." Andrew apologized. He stood with his hands jammed into his pockets, barely looking at Nettie.

"It's okay, it wasn't your fault."

"But I'm still sorry. Drew shouldn't have done that." Andrew shook his head in disgust.

"Yeah, it pretty much sucked." Nettie let out a little laugh.

"We broke up." Andrew's eyes locked with Nettie's.

"I heard."

"So, um, are you really okay? I mean yesterday you took off without telling anyone and I just wanted to make sure that nothing else is bothering you."

"Like what?" Nettie asked, crossing her arms across her chest.

"Like stuff about Joe or your dad." He paused for a moment and took a deep breath. It's now or never, he thought, as he asked, "Or, um, me?"

"What?

"Well, I just thought maybe you needed someone to talk to."

"Did you read my journal, Andrew?" Although he was prepared for that question, it was still difficult for him to have to admit the truth.

"I'm sorry." He hung his head a little. Then he took two steps toward her.

"Oh my God." Nettie backed away.

"I tried not to, I really did. I shouldn't have, I know. I'm so sorry."

"My life is just one big nightmare," Nettie mumbled as she sat on the bed and buried her head in her hands.

"So do you want to talk?" Andrew asked.

"No!" Nettie yelled defensively. "I mean, I guess you already know everything. So, don't worry about it."

"Can I ask you something Nettie?"

"I guess."

"All that stuff you wrote about me, is it true?"

Nettie lowered her head and stared at the ground. "Yes. All of it."

Andrew tilted his head to one side and shoved his hands in his pockets. "So, you do like me?" He smiled.

"I did," Nettie answered quickly.

"But you don't anymore?" Andrew hoped Nettie could hear the disappointment in his voice.

"I … I don't know. What does it matter?"

"'Cause if you do, I thought maybe you'd come with me to the Grad Dance." Nettie stared at him with her mouth slightly open. She looked lost for words.

"So, will you?" Andrew asked again.

"Um, sure." Nettie answered.

"Okay, cool. Well, I gotta go. But I'll see you in school on Monday, okay?" Andrew smiled, and walked out of Nettie's room. He stopped short and turned around. "I almost forgot, I brought this for you." Out of his back pocket Andrew removed a folded, well-worn journal.

"What's this?"

"It's my journal. I thought since I read yours, you know, fair is fair."

"Andrew, you don't have to do this. Really."

"I know. But I want to."

"Well, thanks."

"Sure. See you Monday," he said as he left the room.

"See you." Nettie answered back.

PART THREE
NEW BEGINNINGS

Chapter Twenty-Seven

The Other Side of Lonely

Nettie stood for several moments suspended in thought. Like waking from a dream, she found herself standing in her bedroom clutching Andrew's journal. It was enough of a shock that he'd found her yesterday. It was surreal when he showed up at her house, came in her room, and asked her to the Grad Dance. She wanted someone to pinch her. She looked down at the journal in her hands. For a split second she thought about not reading it. What was the point when she already had what she wanted, Andrew back in her life. But she felt compelled. There was an urge growing within in her. She had to know what was written in the journal. Besides her desire to know, she had a feeling that Andrew wanted her to read it, and not just out of fair play.

She squished herself into her pillows, making herself comfortable, and opened the journal.

Courage

October 26

Today's topic is about courage. We're supposed to either write about a time when we felt courageous or about a courageous person. At first I wanted to write about Joe. Joe was the most courageous person I've ever known. He wasn't afraid of anything or if he was, he never showed it. He always did the right thing. And nothing takes more courage than doing the right thing.

I hardly ever do the right thing. I know what I should do. I know what I want to do, but for some reason, I don't. I always thought that when I grew up I would be just like Joe. I thought it would be easy because he made it look so easy. But I am nothing like him. I'm not the kind of guy who stands up for someone if it means sticking my neck out. I'm not loyal or thoughtful or trustworthy. That takes courage.

I am the least courageous person I know. If I had any courage, I would still have my best friend. But I don't and that's why I lost her.

Nettie blinked back tears as she read. She never knew. She'd always hoped, but she never knew that Andrew felt any sense of loss over not being her friend. She just assumed he never gave it any thought. She read on.

Freewrite

January 14

I've been thinking a lot about high school. I'm more nervous about it then I thought I would be. I'm pretty sure I'll make the football team. It would be nice to make the starting team, but that's going to take a lot of work. Not that I'm not up to it, because I am.

I keep having this dream that I show up on the first day of school with these glasses with tape on them and my hair is gelled to the point of looking shellacked. What if the kids at high school see through me? I don't know what it would be like to have people know the real me. The real me is not someone I let anyone see. Not anymore.

When we were all in kindergarten we were all friends. We didn't laugh at each other or make fun of each other. We just played together. But then something happened and it was like we all had to choose sides. I don't remember picking sides. I just somehow ended up here.

It's because I play sports that I ended up in the popular group. But if they only knew the real me, they'd turn on me in an instant. I'm not cool. I'm not like those guys I see in movies. I'm not confident or cocky. It's all an act. I feel like no one knows the real me.

I have no real friends.

No real friends? What is he talking about? Nettie thought of how Andrew was always surrounded by people. It was as if Charlie and Jake were glued to his side. Not to mention all the girls who followed him around. How could he possibly think he didn't have any friends?

The Future

January 22

What do I hope for the future? Where do I hope to be in twenty years? I have no idea. When I was ten I wanted play high school football, get a scholarship to play college ball, and get drafted by the pros, the same team that Joe played for of course. Then I wanted to marry Nettie and live next door to her brother Joe and my sister Jenna who would also be married. Then we'd raise our kids together just like our parents did. I wanted to live in the same neighborhood we all do now and have a dog named Pete.

I never told anyone that. I just assumed it would happen. I just assumed, because I didn't know that my life was going to change forever. I didn't know that Joe was going to die. Sometimes I think about how that one event changed my entire life and how it's no use to plan for the future because you never know what unexpected thing could ruin it all.

I don't make plans for the future. I don't know where I'll be in twenty years.

Nettie closed the journal. She couldn't read anymore. Reading Andrew's words made her realize that he was suffering too, maybe not in the same way, but he was. Sure Andrew ended up on the cool track while she was the girl most likely to have the back of her skirt tucked into her underwear, but he was still hurting as much as she was.

Nettie realized that Andrew suffered by living in Joe's shadow. He heaped so much pressure onto himself that it must've felt like being buried alive. How can anyone compete with a ghost?

Just then Nettie decided to forgive Andrew. She realized that she too had put too much pressure on him. She hadn't realized it before, but she'd expected him to be like Joe too, and he wasn't, he was Andrew. Before Joe died, Nettie liked Andrew just for who he was. She wondered when that had stopped.

Chapter Twenty-Eight
Big News

Freewrite

April 22

There's only one month left until graduation. I can hardly believe the day is almost here. This week we started working on the Spring Jamboree. Every year it's basically the same thing, each class performs a song and then at the end Missy Davenport sings a solo, "Amazing Grace." Chris offered me the solo, but I turned it down. I'm just not ready to be on stage, in front of people. I did agree to be Missy's understudy and I have the important job of pulling the curtain.

I think my mom and Chris are getting kind of serious. The other day my mom told me she filed for divorce from my dad. He actually sent the papers back signed a few days ago. I cried when she told me. Part of me still wants my dad to come back. I wonder if I always will. I just think he should apologize or explain or something. I doubt there's much chance of that happening.

I'm glad my mom found Chris. She deserves to be happy. We talked for a long time about how both of us deserve to be happy. I think we finally might be moving forward.

As for Andrew and me, things are good. Okay, they're great! We're not a couple or anything, but we've become friends again. We talk on the phone and stuff.

We talk about Joe a lot. I know it's weird, but sometimes when I'm talking to Andrew I feel like Joe is there with me. I love being able to talk about Joe with someone who knew him and loved him as much as I did.

Elisa and Justin are still going out. I finally told her that I was feeling kind of left out so we agreed that no matter who we're dating, we'll always make time for each other. She's my best friend and no boy will ever change that.

I feel like I could totally jinx it by saying so, but things are good.

Nettie came home from Elisa's house to find her mom and Chris waiting for her. Goofy grins stretched across both their faces. Nettie knew right away something was up.

"Hi, sweetheart," Annie said.

Nettie looked back and forth between the two, waiting for an explanation. "What's going on?"

"Chris is staying for dinner."

"Great. And?"

"She's too smart for us, Annie. Go ahead, show her." Annie stretched out her left hand. Her ring finger was sporting a shiny ring.

"Wow. Nice rock, Mom." Nettie inspected the ring carefully, "Good job, Chris."

"So you're all right with this Nettie?" Chris asked.

"I'm great with this." Nettie wasn't quite sure if great was too strong a word, but she knew her mom loved him and that he made her happy. She could get over all the rest.

"So let's celebrate!" Chris hugged Nettie and Annie at the same time. That night at dinner they ate together and laughed together, like a real family.

CHAPTER TWENTY-NINE

MOTHERS AND DAUGHTERS

Nettie dressed for the Spring Jamboree. The green satin dress she and her mother picked brought out the gold color of Nettie's eyes. As she stood in front of the mirror, her mother knocked on the door. "Nettie?"

"Come in." Nettie answered.

"You look stunning," Annie gushed.

"Thanks, Mom."

"Really, you look beautiful, but there's just a little something missing," she said, as she revealed a long, black velvet box.

"Mom, you didn't have to. I haven't even graduated yet. It's just the Spring Jamboree."

"I know. I've wanted to give this to you for a while, and I thought tonight you might want to wear it."

Nettie took the box from her mother as if it were the most precious thing she'd ever held in her hand. She ran her fingers over the velvet, which was worn from age. Nettie traced her fingers over the gold plate with the engraved letters NLT. Nettie LuAnne Turner. The gold, tarnished and discolored, felt cold and a little slimy to the touch. Nettie opened the box. Inside she found her great-grandmother's pearls. "Mom, are you sure? I'm only pulling the curtain in the Jamboree, nothing special."

Annie reached forward and cupped her daughter's head in her hands. "Nettie, you are special. And I love you. You are a talented, beautiful, and intelligent young lady. Even if you are just pulling the curtain, I still want you to have them." She paused and took Nettie's hand in hers. "You look so much like my grandmother. You have her eyes and her smile. Be proud of who you are, Nettie. I am. And I know G.G. and Joe are proud of you too."

She paused for a moment before saying, "Nettie, I know things have been a little hectic lately and maybe I haven't paid as much attention to you as I should, but I'm going to be better at it. I promise. I want to be there for you, no matter what. You can talk to me about anything. You know that, right?"

Nettie nodded. "So as long as we're opening the lines of communication, there's something I wanted to ask you about. And please don't be angry with Chris for telling me. He just assumed you told me and when he found out I didn't know, he felt really bad."

"Mom, what are you talking about?"

"Why didn't you tell me you were taking singing lessons again?"

"I don't know."

"I just wished you'd shared it with me. I want you to share everything with me. Are you keeping things from me because I kept my relationship with Chris from you?"

"No. I swear, Mom. That's not it."

"Then why honey?"

Nettie thought about her answer for a long time. She knew exactly why she'd been keeping it a secret. She knew she would have to tell her mother eventually. So she took a deep breath and began. "Because I'm cursed." Once the words were out of her mouth she felt relieved. She was glad her mother knew the truth.

"What? Nettie, that's ridiculous. You're not cursed." Her mother laughed a little.

"I'm being serious!"

"Sorry. Why are you cursed?"

"Think about it, Mom. Bad things are always happening to me."

"Nettie that's not true."

"It's not? Did anyone else get their journal stolen and photocopied? No. Do you know any other thirteen-year -old who lost their brother and their father? Nope. Just me. It's like the world is always out of control."

"Honey, what do you mean?"

"It's like those rides at the fair. You know the ones that spin real fast and make you throw up? Well, that's my life. Except I'm not even on the ride having fun. I'm just standing there watching everything go around and around."

Nettie continued, "But when it comes to singing, I'm on the ride. I'm the one having fun. And I just didn't want that to end. I didn't want to have to say good-bye to singing, like I've said good-bye to so many other things in my life."

"I think I understand," Annie started, "But Nettie, you have to keep trying. You have to have faith and to believe that good things will happen to you, if you let them. I think what happened to us is that we held onto our pain and that made it impossible to let anything good in. Do you understand what I'm saying?"

"I think I do. I'm just so tired of suffering."

"I'm so sorry that you've had to suffer. I realize I didn't make things easier on you by dating your teacher." They both smiled in agreement. "Nettie, please understand that you are not cursed. We've been dealt a tough hand, but we're still playing. The pain will continue to subside and we will continue to grow and change. Hiding from the world won't make it any less painful. It just makes it lonely. Believe me, I know."

Nettie understood now that her mother had been hiding too, but in different ways. Annie was afraid to move on with her life. Chris had been her first step.

"I'm sorry, Mom. I'll try not to keep any secrets from you from now on." Nettie threw herself into her mother's arms. She knew now that she was still part of the "we." She thought somehow that her mother's moving forward was something she was doing without her. She realized now she was wrong. They were moving on together.

Annie reached into the box and removed the pearls. She unclasped them, placed them around Nettie's neck and refastened them. "Perfect. They look perfect on you." She smiled. Wiping away tears she said, "Okay, let's go."

Chapter Thirty

Center Stage

When they arrived at the Jamboree, Annie headed into the auditorium to find a seat while Nettie started off to her classroom to wait with the rest of her class. From across the school yard, Nettie saw Mr. Campbell running toward her.

"Nettie!" He sounded out of breath.

"What's wrong?" Nettie asked.

"Missy is sick. You have to go on for her." He placed his hands on Nettie's shoulders. "We need you."

"But," Nettie could hardly speak, "I can't."

"Yes, you can. You're the understudy. I wouldn't have cast you unless I thought you could do it. I've heard you sing, Nettie, you're great. Not great, you're outstanding," he gushed.

"*You* think so. But what if I get up there and forget all the words? Or freeze up or something even worse."

"You won't," he assured her.

"Easy for you to say." Nettie started to sweat. Thankfully, she'd given herself a generous helping of Lady Speed Stick.

"Nettie, listen to me. I have faith in you. I believe in you and your talent. You can do this. And you will. Now go warm up. I'm off to tell the principal that there's a change in the program."

With that, he left her standing in the middle of the empty play yard. Stunned, she couldn't move. *This isn't happening. This is a dream.* But it wasn't a dream. It was real. In an hour and a half she would be standing center stage, in front of the entire school singing the closing song, "Amazing Grace." *This is a nightmare. An actual nightmare.*

As if someone else were controlling her limbs, Nettie began to walk forward. She found herself standing in front of the girls' bathroom. She pushed open the door and walked across the ice blue tile floor just as she did at every recess and lunch. She hopped up onto the counter with ease, folded her legs, and stared at herself in the mirror. Her face was pale. She looked like she was about to vomit. After cooling herself with a damp paper towel, Nettie looked at herself again and saw the pearls around her neck. She ran her fingers along them.

She spoke softly to herself, "G.G., Joe. Help me out here. Just this once, can I not make a total fool out of myself? Can I just get up there and do well enough to not be laughed off the stage?"

Just then, the door opened and Elisa entered. "Nettie, what are you doing?"

"Praying."

"Think it'll work?" Elisa smiled.

"It would take a miracle." Nettie climbed off the counter and straightened her dress.

"Mr. Campbell sent me in here to get you. He says he needs you backstage." Elisa walked toward the door and held it open for Nettie.

"Great. Does everyone know yet?" Nettie wiped her face with a paper towel.

"Word is spreading. Anna and Drew were telling everyone." Elisa rolled her eyes in disgust.

Nettie and Elisa knew exactly what Drew and Anna were up to. They were making sure everyone knew about Nettie's solo. That way when Nerdy Nettie took the stage, everyone could be there to watch her fall flat on her face.

Not this time. Nettie left the bathroom with Elisa following behind her. Together they found Mr. Campbell, who looked relieved to see them.

"Ready?" Mr. Campbell asked.

"I guess so," Nettie shrugged.

Nettie stood and watched as the class performances zoomed by. The kindergartners did their usual "Wheels on the Bus" followed by the first graders singing "This Land is Your Land." By the time the sixth graders finished their rendition of "Welcome" from the Disney movie, *Brother Bear,* Nettie's heart began to quicken. Her palms felt clammy and her body itched. She tried her best to stay calm, but it was no use.

The seventh graders left the stage and the eighth graders took their place. The curtain opened and Nettie, as well as her classmates, waited for their cue. Nettie glanced over at the curtain puller. Her replacement, Andrew Wyatt, winked at her. Nettie smiled. She hadn't known he would be taking her place, but seeing him there gave her a feeling of calm.

Mr. Campbell introduced the class and nodded to the pianist, Mrs. Morgan. Mrs. Morgan began to play and together the class sang, "We're All in This Together" from *High School Musical*. The audience applauded and the curtain closed. It was time for the closing solo.

Mr. Campbell again addressed the audience. "Ladies and gentlemen, we have a slight change in our program this evening. Our closing song will be sung by Nettie Gaines." There were a few whispers in the crowd. When the curtain opened, the audience applauded.

Nettie stepped forward and took center stage. She looked again at Andrew, who nodded and smiled with encouragement. Nettie stood at the microphone and surveyed the audience. There were so many people. Someone behind her giggled. Nettie felt every muscle in her body turn to Jell-O. Her knees were weak and she feared they wouldn't hold her. *This is it.*

Mrs. Morgan waited for her cue. Nettie nodded to let her know she was ready. Nettie found her mother in the audience and relaxed a bit. She closed her eyes and drew in all the air her diaphragm could hold. Then she opened her mouth and sang.

Amazing grace, how sweet the sound
That saved a wretch like me.
I once was lost, but now am found
Was blind, but now I see.

The notes were clear and melodious. She never faltered once. The crowd was silent as if nothing existed but Nettie Gaines and her song. The voice of an angel could not have sounded sweeter. Not tonight.

When she finished, there was at first nothing but stunned silence. Soon the crowd erupted in thunderous applause. Nettie stepped to the side of the microphone and with all the grace and dignity in the world, took her bow. *I did it Joe. That was for you.*

It was over. Her misery was over. It didn't matter if they called her Nerdy Nettie ever again. Forget the seventh grade assembly where she had her dress tucked into her underwear. Forget the class composite where she was photographed mid-sneeze. All that was history now. These thoughts swarmed Nettie's head as the audience clapped louder.

They rose to their feet. Some whistled while others made whooping noises. Mr. Campbell made his way toward her. It surprised her when he hugged her, but she hugged him back with all her might. *How will I ever thank him?* Mrs. Morgan handed Nettie a dozen long-stemmed red roses. Nettie, Mr. Campbell, and Mrs. Morgan took three steps backward. Together with the rest of the eighth grade class they bowed again.

And the curtain closed.

CHAPTER THIRTY-ONE
THE DANCE

At exactly 6:30 PM Nettie heard the doorbell ring. *He's here.* Nettie checked herself in the mirror one last time and for the first time felt more than satisfied with her reflection.

Her hair was tied back in a French twist. Her mother had taken her to a salon and had it professionally done. Nettie had never had her hair stacked up on her head quite like this. She looked different, older somehow. Her hazel eyes were rimmed with eyeliner, also a first. Nothing dramatic, just a light brown line. She saw her folded-up glasses on her night table and smiled. *Thank goodness for contact lenses*, she thought.

Nettie descended the stairs with grace and elegance. She had expected that walking in heels would be like Bambi learning to walk. But once she slid them on she felt more like Cinderella. She never tripped once. When she turned the corner and entered the living room, she noticed right away that Andrew's whole face lit up. He smiled at her. She smiled back.

He was dressed in a dark blue suit with burgundy tie. He looked like he'd stepped out of the pages of a magazine. He walked to her and gave her the corsage. White roses. They were perfect.

After what felt like an hour of picture taking, Nettie and Andrew climbed into the back of Mr. Wyatt's car and he drove them to the dance. They sat in silence most of the ride, not because they were uncomfortable, but because they couldn't stop staring at each other. Eventually, they just started laughing. It felt so good to laugh again.

They walked from the car to the gym after Mr. Wyatt dropped them off. Nettie looked around the room. The gym was decorated in a San Francisco theme. Posters of trolley cars and the Golden Gate Bridge covered the walls. In the center of the ceiling hung a huge glittering ball with the words Class of 2007 written across it. Her classmates looked different to her. No longer did she see enemies, she just saw memories. Not all of them good, but all of them added up to this one moment, and surprisingly, she wouldn't change any of them.

Nettie spotted Elisa and Justin together on the dance floor and waved to them. They were a great couple and Nettie was happy for them. She pictured them all hanging out together, watching movies, and she liked the image. She no longer felt like a third wheel around them.

"You wanna dance?" Andrew asked. Startled at first, she relaxed and smiled. She was nervous. He extended his hand and she happily placed hers in it as he guided her onto the dance floor.

They stood apart, not quite knowing what to do next. Andrew stepped forward and put his hands around her waist. Nettie reached up and wrapped her hands around his neck. She felt a strange mix of calm and excitement being this close to him. They swayed to the music, watching the people around them, and occasionally stealing glances at each other.

"You were amazing at the Jamboree." Andrew blushed. "I'd forgotten you could do that."

Nettie laughed. "Me too," she admitted. She knew she could sing. What surprised her was how easy it was to stand on the stage in front of so many people and hear them applaud.

"You look really pretty." Andrew's hands pulled tighter on Nettie's lower back.

Nettie blushed and said, "Thanks." Nettie could hardly stand the excitement. The night could not get any better.

"Nettie." He looked at her in a way he'd never looked at her before. "I'm sorry."

"For what?" Nettie asked, surprised.

"For everything. For not standing by you when I should have. For letting you down."

Nettie could hardly breathe. She'd waited so long for this. "I understand," she replied. The music stopped. She started to pull away but he kept his hands firmly around her waist. "Wait," he said, holding her there against him.

She stopped and waited. "Most of all I'm sorry for never telling you how bad I felt for you after Joe died."

"We were ten, Andrew. It was hard on you too," Nettie reassured him.

"I know, but I should've done more. Joe would've done more. Even at ten, he would've known what to do and what to say." Andrew looked ashamed. "I didn't."

"It's okay, really. Joe wasn't perfect, Andrew. I know he seemed it, but he wasn't. He made mistakes too. It's taken me a while to realize this, but he was really just human. And so are we. Neither one of us has anything to live up to. We just need to be ourselves, and Joe will be proud of that."

Nettie sounded like her mother. But she didn't mind. Joe was their hero, he always would be. But he was also trapped in their memory. He didn't age. He didn't change. It was easy to feel inadequate to a memory. Nettie realized that she and Andrew put so much pressure on themselves to be something they thought they should be. They tried and failed to live up to this impossible standard, all the while forgetting that Joe loved them just the way they were. They needed to learn to do the same.

"I just feel bad that I wasn't strong enough to stand up to my friends. I'm sorry I hurt your feelings." Andrew tilted his head to one side and leaned forward. "I'm also sorry that I never had the guts before to do this."

In front of everyone, at the school dance, in the middle of the gym floor, he kissed her. It was the most public gesture Andrew could've made. Nettie had imagined this moment many times and it far exceeded her expectations. Although she spent countless hours trying to convince herself that she only wanted Andrew as a friend, she knew she felt otherwise. She no longer felt like denying her feelings for Andrew, and the best part was she no longer had to.

The kiss was amazing, like something out of a dream or a movie, only better because it was real. At first Nettie felt as if she were watching everything happen to someone else. But when she opened her eyes, there he was standing in front of her, Andrew Wyatt, the boy she'd known and secretly loved all her life.

Mr. Wyatt picked them up after the dance and Andrew kissed her again, this time on the cheek after he walked her to the door.

Nettie turned to go.

"Will you be my girlfriend?" Andrew asked. Nettie's head whipped around.

"I guess," Nettie answered playfully. Andrew smiled. Then she walked inside and closed the door.

Who am I?

May 31

At first I didn't understand why Mr. Campbell wanted us to write in these journals, but now I think I see. A lot has happened over the last year and I'm really glad that I have this journal to serve as a reminder. Even though there were plenty of rough times this year, I wouldn't change any of it. I used to think that life was something that was happening to me, like I was on the outside looking in. I'm trying to see things differently now. I'm learning that bad things may happen to me, but I choose how I react to them. I can't expect that life will always go smoothly, but I think I'm more prepared to handle the bumps in the road.

The graduation ceremony was amazing. I can't believe it's over. I'll admit, the whole day I waited for my father to make a surprise appearance, but he didn't. I think in my heart I knew he wouldn't, but I couldn't help hoping. I've spent a lot of time waiting for my dad. My mom helped me see that I don't have to wait. If I want a relationship with my dad I can ask for one. I don't have to wait for him to come to me. It never occurred to me that maybe he's scared to reach out to me. But he might be. Maybe I'll write him a letter someday. I'm not ready yet, but maybe soon.

Andrew and I are officially a couple now. We've been together for about three weeks and so far, so good. We talk on the phone a lot and he comes over to hang out sometimes. We're not really allowed to date yet so we watch a lot of movies at my house. Sometimes we even hang out with mom and Mr. Campbell, I mean Chris. It was weird at first, but we're getting used to it.

My mom and Chris are getting married this summer. I didn't expect it to happen so soon, but I guess my mom's tired of waiting too. Once she decided to move on, she went for it, full steam ahead. I'm going to be the maid of honor. I'm pretty excited because Mom has been asking my opinion about everything. I feel like I really am part of the team. The three of us are going to be a family.

Mom and I packed up Joe's room last Saturday. It was hard and we cried a lot, but we agreed—it was time. We each kept one small item and we put the rest in storage. We also donated a lot of his clothes and stuff to the local Goodwill.

Mom is right; it's time to move forward. No more looking back and trying to change the past. It's hard to move on, especially when the past is painful and confusing. I can't say that I'm over Joe's death or my father leaving. I don't know if I'll ever really be over it. But I know now that moving forward doesn't mean forgetting. I know that it's okay to be happy even though they aren't with me.

And that's a start.

The other day I heard this song by The Weepies. It's called "World Spins Madly On." I listened to the lyrics and they reminded me of me. There's this one part that says,

> I thought of you and where you'd gone
> And the world spins madly on

I won't be able to control the things that happen to me. And not all of them will be good. But I've learned to enjoy the ride, to let the world spin, and to have faith that I'll end up in a better place than I started.

The last prompt Mr. Campbell gave us was to again answer the question, "Who am I?" I think I have a better understanding of that question now. I am Nettie LuAnn Gaines. I am thirteen years old, almost fourteen. I am smart and loving and I can sing pretty well. I have a best friend and a boyfriend. I used to say that I was cursed, but I realize now I'm not. I'm just me. The good, the bad, and everything in between. I am Nettie.

Printed in the United States
205427BV00003B/342/P

9 780595 474394